GIRLS ON THE PROWL

THE LIBRARY • THE BURGLAR IN THE RYE • THE BURGLAR ON THE PROWL • THE BURGLAR WHO COUNTED THE SPOONS • THE BURGLAR IN SHORT ORDER

KELLER'S GREATEST HITS

HIT MAN • HIT LIST • HIT PARADE • HIT & RUN • HIT ME • KELLER'S FEDORA

THE ADVENTURES OF EVAN TANNER

THE THIEF WHO COULDN'T SLEEP • THE CANCELED CZECH • TANNER'S TWELVE SWINGERS • TWO FOR TANNER • TANNER'S TIGER • HERE COMES A HERO • ME TANNER, YOU JANE • TANNER ON ICE

THE AFFAIRS OF CHIP HARRISON

NO SCORE • CHIP HARRISON SCORES AGAIN • MAKE OUT WITH MURDER • THE TOPLESS TULIP CAPER

COLLECTED SHORT STORIES

SOMETIMES THEY BITE • LIKE A LAMB TO SLAUGHTER • SOME DAYS YOU GET THE BEAR • ONE NIGHT STANDS AND LOST WEEKENDS • ENOUGH ROPE • CATCH AND RELEASE • DEFENDER OF THE INNOCENT • RESUME SPEED AND OTHER STORIES

BOOKS FOR WRITERS

WRITING THE NOVEL FROM PLOT TO PRINT TO PIXEL • TELLING LIES FOR FUN & PROFIT • SPIDER, SPIN ME A WEB • WRITE FOR YOUR LIFE • THE LIAR'S BIBLE • THE LIAR'S COMPANION

WRITTEN FOR PERFORMANCE

TILT! (EPISODIC TELEVISION) • HOW FAR? (ONE-ACT PLAY) • MY BLUEBERRY NIGHTS (FILM)

ANTHOLOGIES EDITED

DEATH CRUISE • MASTER'S CHOICE • OPENING SHOTS • MASTER'S CHOICE 2 • SPEAKING OF LUST • OPENING SHOTS 2 • SPEAKING OF GREED • BLOOD ON THEIR HANDS • GANGSTERS, SWINDLERS, KILLERS, & THIEVES • MANHATTAN NOIR • MANHATTAN NOIR 2 • DARK CITY LIGHTS • IN SUNLIGHT OR IN SHADOW • ALIVE IN SHAPE AND COLOR • AT HOME IN THE DARK • FROM SEA TO STORMY SEA • THE DARKLING HALLS OF IVY

GIRLS ON THE PROWL
Copyright © 1961, by Lawrence Block
Original Publication, writing as Andrew Shaw

All Rights Reserved. This book or parts thereof may not be reproduced in any form, stored in any retrieval system, or transmitted in any form by any means—spoken, written, photocopy, printed, electronic, mechanical, recording, or otherwise through any means not yet known or in use—without prior written permission of the publisher, except for purposes of review.

Cover & Interior by JW Manus

A LAWRENCE BLOCK PRODUCTION

GIRLS ON THE PROWL

LAWRENCE BLOCK

Chapter One

THE CABDRIVER'S NAME was Rick Noscaasi. He was a short, stubby man with strong arms and bandy legs. He was on the wrong side of forty by a year or two and his hair was beginning to go.

Rick Noscaasi did not mind the slowness of the evening any more than he minded the hectic aspect of the earlier rush hour. As far as he was concerned, he had the best shift of the three conventional shifts. Tips were heavy and traffic was well-nigh non-existent. But it also had its bad points—too many long hauls and too little turnover, and, most important of all, too much chance of a knife in the chest. The number of cabbies with knives in their chests was a little alarming, even to an easy-going guy like Noscaasi.

So to hell with that. Noscaasi had two kids at home who were nuts enough to think he was the greatest thing since Captain Marvel, and a wife who was equally nuts, convinced that he was the finest lover since Valentino kicked off. And his wife, for that matter, was a pretty fine woman. She, too, was on the wrong side of forty, and this took a little of the shine out of her. The woman he slept with nowadays was not quite the same woman he had taken to bed for the first time twenty years ago. The breasts were not firm any longer and the flesh was heavy on the insides of the thighs. Mary Noscaasi could not be described as a raving beauty no matter how cock-eyed you were. But she was his wife and he loved her.

Still, a man is only human. There were times when Rick Noscaasi saw the young girls with their big breasts, the young girls in their summer dresses and high heels, the young girls with the long legs and the blonde hair and the fresh faces. And, like any man with blood flowing in his veins and an aging wife back in the apartment in Parkchester, Noscaasi would think what it would be like with those girls. He would look at their breasts and wonder what it would feel like to hold them in his hands. He would look at their legs and his brain would reel with fantasies of his hands on those legs, his hands stroking those long and shapely legs.

He was human.

But he was a good man, in the full sense of the word, and thinking was as far as it ever went. Perhaps this is not so much a tribute to his husbandly qualities as it might be, for, to tell the absolute truth, Rick Noscaasi was not the type of man who too often had the temptations of the pleasures of the flesh thrust into his face. Women did not fawn over him. Girls did not run after him, begging for his attentions. He was not chased, and, to his credit, he did not chase. That's about it.

Then there was this night in June.

There he was, cruising north, when a girl hailed his cab.

She was not an ordinary girl. This much should be obvious. If an ordinary girl hailed an ordinary taxicab on an ordinary June night in New York City, only a complete dolt would write a book about it. She was a pretty special girl. You could tell this much just by looking at her.

She was a redhead. There are several varieties of redheads. There are redheads with freckled faces and freckled knees and freckled shoulders and, perish the thought, freckled breasts. There are stringbean redheads and fat redheads. One could go on in this vein, but you get the point. There are redheads and there are redheads.

This one was special.

Her skin, to begin with, was creamy. Her hair was a deep, lovely red, and the combination of that very red hair with that very creamy skin was a sight all by itself. The rest of the girl was just as fine. She was tall—about five-nine. She had very big breasts and very long legs and very wide hips and a very narrow waist.

Noscaasi stopped the cab. He turned in his seat and stared at the girl while she opened the back door and sat down in the back seat. She leaned back lazily in the seat and spoke in a quiet, well-modulated voice.

"Central Park," she said.

Noscaasi sighed. "A big place," he said. "Central Park. You got any special part of the park in mind?"

"Just drive through Central Park," the girl said. "Just drive, that's all. Anywhere."

Noscaasi nodded, put the cab in gear and continued north on Eighth Avenue. If the girl wanted to go for a ride, that was fine with him. He wasn't going to argue with her. His flag was down and his meter was ticking and that was all that mattered to him. If the girl wanted him to take her for a joyride in his cab, that was her business.

The cab was passing 52nd Street, making the neatly-timed lights in turn, when he caught sight of her face in the rear-view mirror. It was, as has been reported, an excellent face. He looked at the red hair and the creamy skin. He looked at the lips, red and full, and he looked at the neck and throat. By straightening up in his seat he could see her throat in the mirror all the way to the first pearl button on the lime green blouse.

At 56th Street the light caught him. A bit ashamed of himself but thoroughly nonchalant, Rick Noscaasi adjusted the rearview mirror so that he could see the girl's chest. This made it impossible for him to watch cars behind him through the mirror. This, however, did not bother him. In New York traffic you have to use the side mirror most of the time anyway. And the front of his passenger was more interesting than the cars behind him.

The light turned and he drove on. He found the park entrance at 59th Street and turned into it. The park was fresh and green with the night and he drove slowly but steadily.

Then the game began.

He was watching her in the rearview mirror, studying the

exciting way that her firm breasts pressed out against the sheer fabric of the pale green blouse, when her hands came into play. He watched the hands in the mirror as they moved into position, fastening on the top button of the blouse. The fingers—long, tapered, fingernails painted a deep crimson—toyed with the button. They took a long time at their work. Then, all at once, the button popped open.

Noscaasi caught his breath.

He saw the insides of two perfect globes now, saw the deep V forming between them. The flesh on her breasts was that same perfect and indescribable creaminess and he longed to clutch the girl in his arms, to take hold of her, to press his lips against all that creamy goodness. He wondered how they would feel.

He thought of Mary sitting home, waiting for him, and he flushed with guilt. He tried even to look away from the mirror, to ignore the spectacle of all that lush beauty.

And failed.

The fingers entered the picture again.

Found another button.

Opened it.

And now still more of the girl was exposed to his gaze. Now he saw just how huge her breasts were, saw also how firm they were, how useless a bra would be for a girl built as the redhead in the rear seat was built. The blouse was open almost far enough for him to see her nipples. He could in fact see part of the aureoles that surrounded the nipples, the light tan patches that surrounded pinkness and stood out in sharp contrast on the white skin.

And his mouth watered at the sight. He wanted to see more, to see the girl's full breasts in all their glory. He knew it was wrong, knew that he ought to do his job and forget the temptations the girl was thrusting at him. What the hell was the matter with her, anyhow? For all she knew, he was getting a pretty good eyeful. And you would think a girl would know better. Hell, maybe she was some kind of a nut or something. Wanted to ride through the park just for the hell of it. Wanted the windows wide open. Now she was doing a strip routine. Maybe she was one of those nudists or something.

More buttons.

Then the blouse was off.

If teasing peeks at the girl's teasing peaks had been exciting to Noscaasi, the sight of the breasts completely bared was downright inflammatory. They were just too big and too firm and too white to be true. There was not even a network of blue veins to mar their perfection. The nipples were a deep pink, saucy and inviting, and he watched in fascination as the girl touched each nipple in turn. The nipples stared at him in the mirror and he stared back.

Witch, he thought. She had to know what she was doing, tossing it at him like that. Maybe that was how she got her kicks. Maybe she thought she was being damned cute, getting a guy bothered and then running out and leaving him like that. The rest of the night, he knew intuitively, was going to be hell.

It would be pretty much of an impossibility to keep his mind on his job after what the little redhead in the back seat was doing to his blood pressure.

He could taste her. He could imagine the sensation of those breasts at his lips. He'd been around, he wasn't a kid on his first trip to a five-and-dime funhouse, but he would be damned a dozen times if he'd ever seen a gal with a pair of boobs like those.

And, because there was nothing else to do. He went on calmly driving the cab around Central Park. He knew that he ought to ask her where she wanted to get off. Hell, the meter read a buck and a half already. There was no point in driving her around the park until morning. But at the same time he was willing to end the ride. It was frustrating, it was enough to send a guy to the nut farm, but it was something he couldn't stop. Dammit to hell, he liked to look at her. It wasn't every day that a guy had a chance to stare at boobs like those. It was an evening to remember.

The girl's voice broke the mood.

"Find a place to park," she said.

Noscaasi started to turn around and stare at her, the usual reaction when a fare says something that is profoundly ludicrous. But he remembered in time that this was not the time to turn around and stare at the girl.

Not when she was nude from the waist up.

"A place to park," she repeated. "A nice quiet place where no one will disturb us."

"I don't get it," he said.

"Turn around," the girl said.

He did not move.

"Turn around!"

Her voice this time held the unmistakable edge of command. The cabdriver turned around. The girl sat facing him, her breasts bare, her lips curled upward in a smile. While he stared at her she cupped her breasts in her hands and held them out to him like a peace offering to an angry god.

"Like them?"

He could only nod.

"I'd show you the rest," she said, "but this isn't a very private place. If you'll find a nice private place and park there you'll get to see the rest. And you'll do more than see it. We'll have ourselves a party, little man. A nice party. One you won't forget."

"A parking place?"

"You've got it, little man. Now go park the cab like a nice boy. You'll learn."

He stepped on the gas again and the cab shot forward. His brain was buzzing and he couldn't organize his thoughts. It occurred to him that this was a brand-new way to rob a cab. Get him to park in a secluded place in Central Park, then beat him over the head and grab his money. The thing to do, he decided, was get the hell out of the park and drive to the nearest precinct station. The girl was either a crook or a nut and either way she ought to be locked up for a while.

He found a spot on a rarely used side road and nosed the cab off the grass between a pair of oak trees.

He cut the motor, yanked up the emergency brake. Then he turned to face her again. Her breasts were as pert and saucy as ever. And the same smile remained on her face.

"The back seat," she said. "Come on into the back seat. I'm lonely, little man. Except I don't have to call you *little man* any more. I know your name. It's Rick Noscaasi—it says so on the license there. I was reading it while you were looking at me in the mirror."

He flushed.

"Come on, Rick. Come on in the back seat. I'm all warm for you, Rick."

"There's a blanket," he panted. "A blanket in the trunk. Outside, on the grass—"

"No."

He stared at her.

"I've done it on a blanket," she said. "Loads of times. But I never did it in the back seat of a taxi cab. That's why I want you to come in the back seat, Rick. I'm all burning up, Rick. I'm on fire. And you've got to put out the fire. Now why don't you come in the back seat?"

He was sweating now. The broad was nuts, she was a certifiable nut, but that didn't matter a damn to him. Very little mattered, very little in the world, nothing, in fact, except that there was a half-naked broad in the back seat with the nicest pair of knockers in the western world and she was moaning for him to come join her.

He opened the door, lumbered out of the cab, slammed it, opened the back door and climbed in. She drew away from him, giggling, and then, when he lunged vaguely at her, she caught his face between her two very soft hands and put her mouth very close to his. Her eyes were inches from his own. They were a very deep green.

"Now kiss me," she said.

Her mouth bore down on his and he felt her lips opening, her tongue entering his mouth. He tasted the sweet warmth of her. It lit little fires in his mouth and his heart began to pound against his ribs. Then her tongue withdrew, slowly, sensuously, and his own tongue became the aggressor, slipping past her lips and into her mouth. He tasted her lipstick, minty and fresh. He tasted her soft wet mouth and his brain whirled with dark fantasies.

"Do you like my breasts?" she wanted to know. He didn't have to answer. The light in his eyes supplied her with the answer to her question.

"Then prove it," she challenged. "Make love to them. Show me how much you like them."

He reached out—timid at first, and then more boldly—and he took her big breasts in his hands. His hands were not quite large enough to hold them. But, he thought, it was fun trying. The skin there was soft as silk, soft as satin, and twice as smooth as either. The nipples were hard as red diamonds, pink diamonds, poking exquisite holes in the sweating palms of his hands. He squeezed her breasts and watched passion shoot through her body and bubble in her veins. He squeezed them and she turned into a tiger, a hungry tiger with lust on the brain.

"Kiss them!"

She did not have to ask twice. In fact she would not have had to ask at all, because kissing her breasts was an idea which had already occurred to Rick Noscaasi. Obediently he lowered his lips to one lovely pink-tipped globe. His lips ran over it and planted kisses wherever they landed. Then they closed around the nipple.

"That's it," she moaned. "Kiss it. Keep doing it, I love it, keep doing it, keep doing it, don't stop—"

But she was the one who stopped it. She pushed him away at last while his lips were still swimming with the sweet and indescribable taste of her breasts, pushed him away and, in a single motion, tore her black skirt up over her thighs, over her waist. Her panties were white, lacy, and very sheer.

Her legs were perfect. The same white creaminess, with trim ankles and luscious calves and perfect knees and round thighs.

His hands went to her legs and he began to touch. He ran his hands over her thighs and desire throbbed in him with un-deniable force. No girl had ever been like this one. No legs like these, no thighs like these, no breasts like these. He was no virgin, no mewling adolescent with pimples on his face and a changing voice and sex on the brain. He was a grown man— but this girl was enough to turn him into a boy again.

His hands were on her knees. Slowly they coursed upward, feeling the sweet texture of the skin of her thighs, moving higher. The girl began to squirm. Her head was thrown all the way back so that it rested on the armrest of the far door. Her breasts stood up straight and proud.

She squirmed.

Noscaasi did not have to be told what to do. His fingers curled beneath the elastic band at the top of her white lacy panties. Slowly, tantalizingly, he drew the panties down over her hips and thighs. He took them off and dropped them to the floor of the cab.

He touched her. With masculine ingenuity half-forgotten he touched her and turned her into a raging demon. He didn't need these tricks with Mary. When he and Mary slept together they did so as a matter of course. After twenty years of marriage little subtlety remained.

Now he was clever with his hands. Now every gesture drove the girl to a higher peak.

Her mouth dropped open. She sat up now, her eyes dripping desire and she reached for him.

It did not take long. She trembled. Then she flung herself down on the seat of the car once again, her body vibrating from head to toe.

"Make love to me," she begged. "I want it, I need it, I have to have it. Don't wait, don't stop, just make love to me, damn it!"

And he fell upon her.

The rear seat of any car, including a taxi, is not constructed for horizontal pleasantries. With the exception of the Nash, in which both the seats and the passengers go down at will, an automobile is ill-disposed to be a party to amorous congress. Yet the surprising number of affairs consummated every year in the back seats of automobiles—and, occasionally, even in the front seats—bears witness to the fact that certain obvious advantages offset the difficulties involved in automotive love.

There is the accessibility, for one thing. Not everyone has a private apartment at his or her disposal. Not everyone can afford the price of a hotel room. And, for another thing, a girl whose pride would not permit her to check into a hotel can be coaxed into submission in a car.

These factors had nothing to do with what was going on in the back seat of the taxi which was piloted eight hours out of every twenty-four by one Rick Noscaasi. This taxi was being used for one reason.

It was there.

And so, for that matter, were they. Noscaasi and the redhead. There they were.

He threw himself upon her and her breasts cushioned his fall and her body surrounded him, welcoming him. He wished for one shadow of time that he had taken the trouble to remove his shirt. It would have been nice to feel her breasts bulging against his chest. For that matter, it would have been nice to disrobe so that he could feel her body on his.

He did not concern himself with such matters for long.

Because she was ready for him and ever so gently it was beginning.

It went slowly at first. It was hard for him to contain himself, hard for him to make it take as much time as it could. He had a great desire to do it quickly, to finish it almost before it got started, to abandon himself to the sweet thrill of fulfillment without making a big production out of it.

But he restrained himself. He knew instinctively that this was something which was happening now and which would never be repeated. He knew that he would probably never see this redheaded passion-pot again and that he would almost undoubtedly never have her again like this.

He wanted to make it last.

So it went slowly at first. Slowly, with their passion building gradually and growing with every slow and gentle movement.

Slowly.

His hands found her breasts again and held them. His hands flexed those breasts and he wanted to squeeze hard, to make her scream with a combination of passion and pain. He satisfied himself with pinching the pink nipples and teasing them into passionate awareness.

Slowly.

Then more rapidly.

With his body doing things he hadn't known it could do.

Faster.

Still faster.

The world began to spin and shake and fall apart. Colors

swam before his eyes and his heart pounded in his chest and he thought that his heart was going to burst, that his body could not withstand the devastating force of passions like these. But he could not stop, could not slow down the progress of what the two of them were doing.

Faster—

And her voice rang in his ears:

"Do it, little man. Do it. I love it, Mr. Cabdriver, Lover, whoever you are. I love it, don't ever stop!"

Faster—

He was not in his forties now. He was not a broken-down driver of a broken-down cab, a mousy married man with tired blood and hardening arteries.

He was something else entirely.

He was transfigured. He was young now, a young man who stood six foot three in stocking feet, a young man with the physique of a Greek god and the musculature of a statue by Michelangelo. He was Manhood—harsh and undeniable, strong and irresistible, potent and irrefutable.

He was hell on wheels.

Faster—

The world turned upside-down and inside-out and swallowed itself. He gasped and the peak was there for him and for her. His body shook and churned in fulfillment.

It was over.

THE GIRL PULLED herself together. She pushed her skirt down over her thighs, picked up her blouse and struggled into it, buttoning it over her breasts. She sat up on the seat and looked through her purse for a comb. She combed her long red hair until it was as it had been before.

Then she turned to him.

"Snap out of it," she said. "That was nice but it's over now. It was very nice, as a matter of fact. I'm sorry I called you Little Man before. It was a mistake. A grave mistake. There's nothing remotely little about you."

He looked stunned, she thought. She felt like laughing but she controlled herself.

"Now get in the front seat," she said. You've got to drive me out of here."

He seemed numb, but he managed to follow orders. He got out of the cab, walked around to the front, hopped in and got behind the wheel.

"Where to?"

She hesitated a moment. She did not want to give him her address. While he had been amusing, she certainly did not intend to see him again. And he might be annoying if he knew her address. He might drop around, or start camping on her doorstep, or something like that.

She did not want that.

"Just take me out of the park," she said. "Anywhere. 59th Street, say. I can manage from there."

"I can take you home. No trouble."

"59th Street is fine."

He accepted that. He started up the car and drove. She

settled back into the seat and relaxed. It was easy to relax now. There was nothing quite like a good session with a man to help you relax. Nothing like that. A little grinding of the hips, a little panting, and life was a hell of a lot easier to take.

Her name was Sandra Stone. When she attended high school in Scarsdale they called her Sandy Stone. When she went to Clifton College they improved on this and called her Sandstone, making a single word out of it. Now, in New York, she had added a letter to her name and called herself Saundra.

Saundra Stone. She leaned back now and looked out the window at the night while Rick Noscaasi's cab found its way along the twisting roads of Central Park to 59th Street. The cab got there, finally, and she sat upright in her seat. She noticed that he had left the meter off. That was good. She did not intend to pay him anything, of course, and he would only have to make up the difference if he ran the meter.

"Stop here," she said.

The cab pulled to the curb. He turned and looked at her, a long look that she could not entirely decipher. She opened the door of the cab and stepped out onto the street.

"Hey," he said.

She wanted to walk away. But she stopped and went back to the cab.

He was pointing to the floor of the back seat. Her panties lay there in a tangled heap.

"You keep them," she told him brightly. "Tuck them under your pillow for a souvenir. Every time you see them you can remember me and dream happy dreams."

She walked away from him then and a smile played on her lips. She kept walking—a few seconds later his cab passed her as he cruised and looked for another fare. He was shaking his head and his expression was puzzled.

She laughed.

She crossed 59th Street and walked down two blocks to Sixth Street where a luncheonette beckoned to her. She had a plate of waffles and bacon and a cup of hot chocolate. Sex always improved her appetite. She wolfed the food down greedily, drank the chocolate, paid her check and left a good tip for the waitress. Then she went out into the night and caught the first cab she saw.

"105 East 73rd Street," she told the driver. She sank into her seat without taking any notice of him and relaxed again. She closed her eyes, savoring the memory of the affair in the park, and opened them when they were in front of her building.

The meter read sixty cents. She handed the driver a single and told him to keep the change.

The doorman held the door for her. He said: "Good evening, Miss Stone." She smiled briefly at him and went to the elevator. The elevator operator also wished her a good evening and whisked her to the floor. She left the elevator, went to her apartment and knocked. Someone called for her to come in and she did.

It was a good apartment. Four rooms, good furniture, high ceilings, thick wall-to-wall carpeting. It should be good, she thought. It rented for $210 a month. Her end of that was seventy dollars.

Another girl walked into the living room. She was a few inches shorter than Saundra. Her hair was black and she wore it short. Her figure was excellent. Her breasts were a little smaller than Saundra's, but this was to be expected. The same could be said for almost all girls.

"Where's Joan?"

"Out," the brunette girl said. Her name was Marilyn Harper. "Pull up a chair. Relax."

Saundra pulled up a chair and relaxed.

"You're positively glowing," Marilyn said. "What have you been up to?"

"Nothing much."

"Come on—tell Mama."

Saundra smiled. "Nothing, really. I got in a cab and told the cabby to take me to Central Park. Then he got in the back seat."

"How was it?"

"It was fun."

"Of course it was," Marilyn said. "I told you it would be. It's always fun."

Chapter Two

THE THEATER WAS small—twenty rows of twelve wooden chairs each, divided by a center aisle. It was on Commerce Street, in the western part of Greenwich Village. The play currently being performed was entitled *A Sound of Distant Drums*. It was a heavy but amateurish thing, loaded with symbolism and devoid of ideas, and it was coming to the end of a brief and not at all spectacular run.

Less than half of the one hundred twenty seats were occupied this Thursday evening. Of those, twenty or thirty had been bought and paid for—by idiots, no doubt. The remaining were occupied because the management, in a heroic attempt to transform a turkey into a hit, had engaged in the simple expedient of papering the house—that is, flooding the western world with free tickets.

The recipient of one of these tickets, a pretty blonde wearing a loden green suit, was sitting in the third row on the aisle. Her name was Joan McKay.

The distant drums were on the way out now—soon they would not be sounding at all. For this Joan McKay was duly grateful. The play was an incredible bore, so much so that although her ticket had cost her nothing she still felt the evening was over-priced. If she'd had any sense, she thought, she would have left during the intermission. One act was enough for anyone, no matter how masochistically inclined the theater-goer might be. Two acts was torture.

If somebody wanted to write a play, she thought, he could do worse than turn to the three of them for inspiration. They could call it *Three Little Maids From School*, she thought. Saundra and Marilyn and Joan. Three little maids from various schools, actually. Saundra from Clifton, Marilyn from Michigan, herself from Wessex. A trio of girlish graduates at loose in the Big City.

She looked briefly at the stage, shuddered and went back to her line of thought. Vaguely she wondered what the other two were doing at that moment. They probably had men up at the apartment, she guessed. It was not a difficult guess to make. They *generally* had men at the apartment, or else they were at some man's apartment, or something. Sweet Lil Ole Marilyn and Sandstone might not be nymphomaniacal, exactly, but they were working at it. They were starring in a strange morality play about girls on the loose in New York, and, strangely enough, it was Michigan's Marilyn who was leading Scarsdale's Saundra down the primrose path.

Not that Sandstone had been so damned pure to begin with. Clifton was supposed to be a pretty sexy school, and Joan had no doubt that Saundra had gotten her fill there. But Marilyn was exceptional, damn it. It wasn't exactly that she had her brains set snugly between her knees. She had brains in her head, all right. She was a whip—high grades in school, a keen mind, enough ambition so that she was moving along in her job at Phulcorte Press. She'd made the jump from editorial assistant to assistant editor already, and soon she'd be in line for associate editor, and that was a lot of distance to cover in a year.

It was more a case of having her brains in her head but, at the same time, doing a fair measure of thinking with her desires. That was it, Joan decided. Something had gone a little wrong with her sympathetic nervous system. She had two minds, a cerebral mind and an amorous one. Magnificent.

And Saundra was doing her damnedest to follow Marilyn's example. Her amorous example, that is. Not her cerebral example, because Saundra Stone didn't seem to care at all about getting ahead in the business world. She plodded along, pounding a typewriter for Caution Insurance and taking home a steady sixty-two-fifty a week, and waited to catch the right husband. Physically she followed in Marilyn's footsteps. They both seemed determined to share at one time or another, the bed of every male in New York. An impossible ambition, Joan thought. But at the rate they were going they just might fulfill it.

And she was rooming with them, sharing the plush apartment on East 73rd Street. That was what was so funny. If any girl did not fit in with Marilyn and Saundra, it was her. She was so out-of-place that her non-conformity was a ready topic of breakfast-table discussion. She was the outlander, the quiet one, the wearer of the chastity belt. She was the one who was not only not promiscuous but, incredibly, sexually inert. No man had ever made love to her at Wessex. No man had ever made love to her in New York. No man had ever made love to her, period.

Marilyn and Sandstone called her the Vestal Virgin.

If they only knew—

Half of the audience was applauding politely, and the cast took that as a signal to indulge in three highly unwarranted curtain calls. Then the curtain dipped for keeps, the house lights came up and a bored usherette with a black ponytail and too much makeup under her eyes opened the door and let the poor audience escape into the night.

Joan McKay walked east on Commerce Street, heading toward Seventh Avenue. She was a very pretty girl. Her shoulder-length blonde hair was done up in a pert bun that nestled prettily on the back of her head. Her eyes were a cool blue, her features distinctive and good. She was about five-five and built well. Firm breasts thrust out against the jacket of the loden suit. Good legs moved quickly and easily as she walked along. She wore seamless nylons and nut-brown wedgies.

Now you go home, she told herself. You walk up to Sheridan Square, catch a local to Times Square, shuttle to Grand Central, ride home on the Lexington IRT. You take a hot bath and read for a while.

But she did not turn north on Seventh Avenue. Instead she

crossed the wide street and continued east on Bleecker, passing Italian food stores and a pizza place and a shoe repair stand and a candy store. She walked at the same speed as before but there was something different in her stride now. Anticipation, perhaps. Excitement.

She worked from nine to five, Monday through Friday, as a proofreader for *Agony*, a literary quarterly that limped along financially and attempted to bring bright new stars in the sky of literature to the breath-bated public. Since *Agony* paid its contributors with subscriptions to the magazine, and since its readership was optimistically estimated at seventy-five hundred, this attempt was not too successful. Still Joan enjoyed her work. The people she met were interesting people, filled with ideals of one sort or another, and the work was simple enough. When she was not reading proof she functioned as a sort of first reader, screening out the bilge and mailing it back to its hopeful authors while adding their names to the magazine's mailing list, passing on the possible contributors to Harvey Chase. Harvey was editor and publisher of *Agony*, and the brains behind the magazine, if the magazine had indeed any brains at all behind it.

This is what she did for a living. An easy and interesting job with a small but sufficient paycheck. This, however, was not on her mind at the moment.

She was thinking of something else.

I shouldn't do this, she thought angrily. I shouldn't, I really shouldn't, I'm being a damned fool again. I'm always being a damned fool, I've got to get control of myself, sublimate or something, find a way to cool off.

Turn around, get the subway, go home. Go home go home go home go home—

She turned on Cornelia Street. It was a street which the Village's army of tourists rarely noticed. Quiet, ordinary in appearance, residential. She walked to the middle of the block where an almost invisible wooden board spelled out the name of the sole commercial establishment on the block.

Open d'Or.

She walked down the stone stairway to the door, which was *not* open, as it happened. She opened the door and walked inside. There was a residue of sawdust on the floor, a combination of a corny attempt at atmosphere and an excuse for leaving the floor unswept. Otherwise the room was unremarkable. A dimly-lit bar. A dozen scattered tables, topped with red and white checked tablecloths. A long brown bar with a dozen stools. A juke box in the back, a slow, sad Dinah Washington record playing. Bottles and glasses and brittle voices.

She found an empty stool with empty stools on either side of it and took a seat at the bar. The barmaid, a short girl with black hair done in an Italian-style ducktail haircut, came over to take her order.

"A stinger," she said.

I could have had a stinger for seventy cents on Sheridan Square, she thought. And it would have tasted just as fine, and the bar would have been nicer and the air fresher. But here I am.

The Vestal Virgin. Chastity personified, Santayana's last puritan, with interest. Sweet, twenty-two, and never been deflowered.

Sitting in a lesbian bar and waiting for a pickup.

They did not know, of course. She was positive of that. Marilyn and Saundra, secure in their indisputable heterosexuality, couldn't suspect that their chaste little roommate was gay as a jay. For one thing, she did not look the type. Not with her large breasts, not with her feminine walk. In short, she did not look like a butch, a mannish lesbian. And, in most people's minds, all lesbians are butch types.

Nor did she act like a dyke. It was difficult at times in that cozy little lovenest on East 73rd Street. It was hard as nails, especially with Sandstone and Marilyn walking around in next to nothing half the time and talking sex the other half. If they were unattractive girls it would have been easier. But they were not, not by any stretch of the imagination. They were very lovely and eminently desirable. And Joan desired them.

That was the bad part. Sitting in the apartment while Saundra sat across from her in bra and panties, with those beautiful legs bare and those huge and perfect breasts ready to explode through the flimsy and unnecessary bra. Sitting in the apartment while Marilyn, fresh and moist and sweet smelling from a shower, waltzed around naked and patted herself dry with a nubby yellow towel. At least the girls had separate bedrooms, and Joan thanked God for that. If she had to share a bedroom with either of them it would be too much for her to stand.

Sometimes it got so bad she would itch and burn with want for one or the other of the girls. Sometimes it became a genuine physical ache. Fortunately it was strictly physical and no more than that. She was not in love with either. In fact, she had not been in love since her junior year at Wessex. Marna—hot, breathless, beautiful Marna.

But that was long ago.

She took a sip of her drink. It tasted fine. As she was setting the drink down she became aware of the girl sitting beside her.

She turned her head.

"Drink up," the girl said. "So I can buy you a refill."

The girl was probably a year or two or three older than Joan. Her hair was dark brown, her eyes very dark. She was wearing a bulky boatneck sweater which concealed her figure from the world. Her face was very thin, her mouth a red slash, her eyes hollow with dark circles under them If you saw her on the street in a small town in Idaho you would not for a minute suspect that she was a lesbian. In a gay bar in the Village it was more than obvious. Placed in her proper setting, the Open d'Or, she looked like a lesbian. There was some indefinable thing about her which made her abnormality unmistakable.

"My name's Terri," she said. "Terri Hall. I don't think I've seen you around before. Do you come down here often?"

"Once in while," Joan said. *When I have to*, she thought.

"But you live uptown?"

"That's right."

"I live a few blocks from here," Terri said.

Joan didn't say anything.

"On Gay Street," Terri said. She forced a smile.

The familiar feelings began to build in Joan's body. She felt the tensions returning, the hungers reappearing. She wanted to find out what Terri looked like with the sweater off. She wanted to know the flavor of Terri's mouth, the warmth of Terri's body.

She finished her drink. The dark-haired girl motioned to the barmaid, pointed at Joan's empty glass. "And bring me rye and soda, Lee," she said.

The barmaid made the two drinks. Terri put two singles on the top of the bar. They picked up their glasses, clinked them together, and drank.

The first drink was working now, Joan noticed. Her head was the least bit light, her mouth the least bit dry. It was working. The rest would follow easily enough.

"I don't think I got your name, honey."

"Joan," she said. "Joan Barton."

No connections. No affairs. Never give your right name, don't let them know who you are. Live uptown, live your own life. Come downtown for sex. Not love, not friendship, not even companionship. Just sex.

"You like this place, Joan?"

"It's a bar."

"It's noisy," Terri said. "My apartment's a lot quieter. We could be alone there."

And to make things as obvious as possible her hand settled on Joan's thigh and squeezed. Joan thought the gesture was unnecessary, gauche. But it excited her nevertheless.

"I'd like to see your apartment," she managed.

"As soon as we finish this drink."

They picked up their glasses.

MARILYN HARPER PICKED up the phone in the middle of the third ring. She was sitting in a chair next to the table on which the phone reposed and could have answered it at once, but that was not the way she did things. Answer right away and they think you're over-anxious. She did not want anyone to think she was over-anxious.

"Hello," she said. "Who's this? Just a minute—I'll see if she's in."

She turned to Saundra, the mouthpiece cupped in one hand. "Some joker named Frank Ralston. Sounds like a cereal. Are you in to him?"

Saundra was. She took the phone from Marilyn and held it to her ear. "Hi, Frank," she said. "How are you?"

Marilyn's mind roamed. She was frankly tired and frankly bored. The past four days at Phulcorte Press had taken a lot out of her. Marilyn was a girl who threw herself into her job with a vengeance. She got to work early and left late. She took short lunch hours. She worked hard and kept busy. Tomorrow was Friday, the last day of work before the blessed respite of the weekend. It was going to be damned difficult to get to work tomorrow. She did not want to go to work. She wanted to sleep late and wake up with a man in bed next to her. Then she wanted to spend the day in bed, doing a myriad of delightful things with the man.

Instead she would go to work. And it would be a bore.

She scratched a match and lit a cigarette. It was close to midnight and there was nothing worth watching on television. The late movies were all dogs. Why she didn't go to bed was a damned fine question. She knew the answer. She wasn't going to bed now because she couldn't possibly sleep. She was far too tense to sleep.

Saundra's little story about the evening's entertainment certainly hadn't done anything to relax her. Sandstone was quite a storyteller. She'd given every last detail of the passionate encounter with the sweaty little cabby, and the details had only made Marilyn more aware of her own need for a man.

Not that she hadn't wanted the details. If you couldn't have love, the next best thing was vicarious love. If you couldn't get it, the next best thing was a glowing account of what Saundra had received. If you couldn't be doing it you could at least be thinking about it. There were two important aspects to Marilyn Harper's life. One was work and the other was loving. You involved yourself in one or the other at all times, unless you were asleep. In which event you dreamed—about work or about love. Those were the only two fields worth dreaming about.

When Marilyn involved herself in something she held

nothing back. That was why she was moving so spectacularly at Phulcorte. Another month or two and she'd be an associate editor. She had plenty on the ball and the higher-ups knew it. And a few months after that and Phulcorte wouldn't be able to hold her. It was too minor an outfit. The only place to go from an associate slot was a full editorship and they didn't have room for her there. She'd find another outfit, one with more growing space.

She worked like a Turk. And there was only one way she could relax, only one way she could escape the constant pressure of the job. That was sex. Sex—hot and fast and intense and passionate—provided her with her sole means of escape. The release of loving was the only release open to her. She loved as she worked. She threw herself into it completely, and no girl on earth enjoyed it more thoroughly or performed more competently.

Now Saundra was hanging up the receiver. Marilyn broke off her train of thoughts and looked up. "Well?" she said.

"Frank Ralston," the redhead said.

"The cereal king," Marilyn said. "That much I know already. Who is he and what did he want?"

"He's a guy."

"Thanks a lot."

"He's a friend of Jim Schwerner. I met him at a party a couple of weeks ago. That blast over on the West Side. I think I told you about it."

"The one where you wound up in Harlem?"

"That's the one. Anyway, I met Frank at the party. He didn't come uptown with the rest of us. He called just now to ask me out for tomorrow night. He has tickets to a fight at the Garden."

"That sounds about as exciting as a turtle race."

Saundra shrugged. "I like boxing," she said. "And he has ringside seats. So I told him I'd like to go."

"Dinner, too?"

Saundra shook her head. "He's picking me up after dinner."

"You're nuts, you know."

"Why?"

"He calls at the last minute. He doesn't even ask you out for dinner. You could play a little harder to get, Sandstone. You make it too easy."

"Look," Saundra said, "he's just a guy. He's a nothing at an ad agency. He makes a staggering six or seven thousand a year. Why play hard to get? I'm not going to marry the jerk. I'm just going to the fights with him. That's all."

"Going to sleep with him?"

"Probably."

"Why?"

"He's good-looking. With luck he'll be good in bed."

"You're looking for a husband," Marilyn said. "A rich husband. God knows why—your folks are respectably upper-middle-class Westchesterites. You don't *need* to marry rich."

"But I want to."

"You want to," Marilyn echoed. "So why waste your time

on a guy you wouldn't marry on a bet? Why not hunt the rich sucker instead of marking time with Frank Cheerios?"

"Ralston."

"Frank Pablum, for all I care. But why?"

"I told you. He's a nice guy."

"That makes sense."

"It makes sense to me," Saundra said. "I'm not like you, Marilyn. You pick a goal and shoot straight toward it. That's not the kind of person I am. I have to sort of feel my way along. I do things because I want to do them. I want to go out with Frank because I *want* to, that's all. Not because he'll turn into a rich husband. Because it'll be fun."

Marilyn shrugged.

"The hell with it," Saundra said. "I don't want to argue. Anything on television?"

"Nothing."

"I don't feel like watching it anyway. Where the hell is Joan, anyway?"

"God knows. Probably sitting in a coffeehouse downtown and talking about capital-L literature with a passel of intellectuals. That's her speed."

"And capital-L life and capital-L love."

"You've got it." Marilyn laughed. "The Vestal Virgin seeking after truth. With a capital T yet. She could learn a hell of a lot more in bed."

"With a capital B," Saundra said.

*   *   *

JOAN WAS NOT in bed, with or without a capital B. She was, however, *on* a bed. The bed was Terri's; it was the only really comfortable place to sit in the dark-haired girl's one-room fourth-floor walkup apartment on Gay Street. There was an easy chair with busted springs and a straight-backed chair with an air of austerity about it. She and Terri were both seated on the bed drinking room-temperature sherry out of paper cups.

A Haydn string quartet rotated pleasantly on Terri's lo-fi portable phonograph. So did the room. Two stingers and several sips of sherry had brought Joan to just the right plateau of semi-intoxication. Drowsy but not sleepy, high but not dizzy, happy but not giggling. She felt fine.

At first there had been an overhead light, a single bulb that dangled glaringly from the ceiling. But Terri had turned the bulb out and switched on a small table lamp in its place. The lamp had a dim red bulb—a bit phony, but nice when you were a little bit high, a wee mite stoned.

She turned to Terri.

"Joan—"

Her name whispered in a husky, throaty whisper. She always gave her right first name to the girls who picked her up. It would be horrible to be called by someone else's name.

She leaned forward, setting the paper cup with an inch of sherry still in it upon the floor. She sat up again, turned once more to face Terri. Her heart was beating wildly and she wanted to hold Terri in her arms, to taste Terri's mouth, to feel the other girl's warm body press against her.

But first Terri tossed off her own wine. Then she smiled, her eyes clouding with passion, and then, slowly, she leaned forward. Her face was beautiful in the warm glow of the red-bulbed lamp. The deep hollow eyes. The sharp chin. If Modigliani had been a female homosexual he would have painted Terri.

They leaned slowly together, bodies touching, mouths meeting in a kiss. It was a strangely chaste kiss, giving the lie for the moment to the passions both of them felt. Joan felt the girl's arms go around her, felt hands on her back.

Both mouths opened together. Terri was the aggressor but she was a gentle aggressor, a subtle rapist. Her tongue was a feather that caressed Joan's lips, a warm wet feather that slipped between the parted lips and touched the teeth and dipped deep, tasting of rye and sherry and passion, bringing warmth and pleasure and desire. Now Joan's arms were around the dark girl, drawing her close, holding her against her. Through the double thickness of her own jacket and Terri's bulky boatneck sweater she felt softness and firmness, the softness and firmness of two breasts touching her own breasts.

The kiss ended and they parted. "It's warm," Terri said, her voice still a whisper, and then Terri was taking off her sweater, drawing it over her head, while Joan removed her own suit jacket. Both wore almost identical white blouses. Terri's was monogrammed, and Joan was glad that hers was not. The initials would have differed with those of the name she had given the girl.

They kissed again. This time the fervor of Terri's embrace carried Joan over, literally bowled her over, and she was lying down on the bed with Terri leaning over her, their mouths still locked in a kiss. She took Terri's face between her own hands and sent her tongue deep into Terri's mouth, taking up sweetness and warmth, drinking passion.

Terri's hands touched her breasts, warm through the blouse and bra. Terri began to caress the firm flesh and Joan's whole body responded to the insistent caress of those devilish hands. She was breathing deeply now and the palms of her hands were moist with desire. The desire was not at all unilateral. Beads of sweat stood out on Terri's brow and her eyes were shining.

With dexterous fingers Terri unbuttoned Joan's blouse and pulled it loose from the skirt. Joan lifted herself up on her elbows so that Terri could reach around her body and unhook her bra. The action pressed their bodies together and the contact was electric. Once again they were locked in a kiss, mouths together, hearts pounding. When the kiss ended and they separated Joan was no longer wearing a bra.

"They're so beautiful, baby. So nice, so sweet. And you want me. I can tell that you want me, the way your nipples stand up so straight and tall. Pretty pink nipples. Nice little nipples. Your breasts are bigger than mine, Joan. I love them."

Terri's hands now moving skillfully and magnificently on her bare breasts, sending small sweet jets shooting through every bit of her body. Terri's fingers drawing circles around her nipples and making her skin crawl with hunger.

She had to be active now, had to play a part. Her own hands opened the buttons on the front of Terri's blouse, drew the blouse over the girl's shoulders, unhooked the bra and took it off. Terri's breasts were small but very well shaped, little inverted bowls. She took them in her hands and caressed them and watched the results of her action mirrored in Terri's hot dark eyes. She squeezed and relaxed and Terri's little nipples jutted against the palms of her hands.

"Lie on me," she urged. "I want to feel you against me."

She stretched out now, kicking off her shoes and extending her legs on the bed. Terri lay above her, her mouth pressed to Joan's mouth, her breasts touching Joan's breasts. The sensation was almost too exciting. Joan's body churned automatically in the motions of love. She could not contain herself.

"We don't want to muss our skirts, Joan. Let's take them off."

In no time at all they both had their skirts off. Joan took off her garter belt, unrolled her stockings. Terri was wearing white wool socks. She took them off.

Now they both wore only panties. And when they stretched out again, the excitement they had known before was more than trebled.

"Relax," Terri was urging her. "Relax, close your eyes, don't move. Just relax."

It was not an easy set of instructions to follow. She wanted to move, to act. But she did as Terri said. She let her eyelids drop shut, made her arm and leg muscles go limp. It was hard at first but it became easier. There were many ways to love. One was to submit, to submit completely, to lie very still and be caressed. She did this.

Terri moved away from her and for a moment she was alone. Then, Terri's hands were stripping her panties slowly down. She was naked then and she felt strangely exposed. It was almost bad for a split second. Then Terri was touching her again and it was all right.

Terri kissed her closed eyelids, kissed her cheeks, kissed the tip of her nose. Terri's mouth planted fleeting kisses all over her face, kissed mouth and chin, kissed everywhere.

Then her throat. She felt the pulse beating in the hollow of her throat and then she felt Terri kissing the spot, her mouth open, her kisses warm. Terri trailed a column of kisses over one shoulder, marched a twin column of kisses over the other shoulder. Terri's lips went out and coursed down into the valley between Joan's breasts.

Joan was spinning now. It was good, very good, and when Terri began to kiss her breasts it got even better. Much better.

She felt Terri's mouth, lips slightly parted, on the downy-soft underside of one breast.

Joan shivered. Terri's lips were closing around her nipple now. The dark-haired girl was kissing the nipple, charging Joan's system with electrical sensations, making her burn alive with aching need.

A pause.

Joan's hands were knotted into small fists now, her arms

wrought iron bands at her sides, her legs tense from warm thighs to pointed toes. She wanted to cry out, to scream with a mixture of want and excitement.

Terri again, Terri's mouth, Terri's lips. Every time that Terri kissed her, still another part of her body began to burn with a hard blue flame.

Lower.

Lips, Terri's lips, moving with aching slowness over her like the fingers of a connoisseur caressing a golden bowl.

Lower.

And then it all began, everything, everything there was, and Joan tangled her fingers in Terri's hair and screamed into the black night.

Chapter Three

HENRY JACKSON, WEARING white trunks with a black stripe, landed a left hook high on the jaw of Tony Giardenieri, wearing black trunks with a white stripe. That, at any rate, is how a television announcer would have explained it. Television announcers are color-blind except when it comes to trunks. In the minds of the bulk of the viewers, the nigger hits the white boy in the face. Other viewers, notably those located in the approximate neighborhood of 125th Street and Lenox Avenue, would say that the spade hit the fay cat in the face. It's all your point of view. What it boiled down to, fundamentally, is that Henry Jackson a Negro, hit Tony Giardenieri, a Caucasian, high on the jaw with a left hook. Giardenieri retaliated by hitting the canvas.

That was that.

Saundra Stone was breathing hard throughout the referee's mournful count to ten. The three preliminary bouts, characterized by inept punching and general lack of coordination, had had little effect on her. The main event, interrupted now in the seventh round by Jackson's knockout of Giardenieri, had been different. Her heart was beating very rapidly and she couldn't quite catch her breath.

Saundra was a fight fan in much the same manner most women are fight fans. The fine points of the contest were lost on her. She was more likely to ooh or ahh over a powerful wallop that landed on the recipient's glove than a short, deadly in-punch thrown in a clinch. She enjoyed the fights, not because she really knew or cared what was happening in the canvas coffin, but because she liked to watch two strong and able-bodied men knock hell out of each other. It was a spectacle which rarely failed to enchant her.

If you had told Saundra that she was sadistic she would have been deeply offended and more than a little disturbed at the notion. She didn't like to hurt people. She nearly cried when an airplane crashed and she read about it in the paper, or when a man was pinned under a car, or something like that. Yet she enjoyed prizefights, and her enjoyment was distinctly sexual and obviously an outlet for a small streak of latent sado-masochism in her make-up.

People were getting up to leave. She turned to the man seated next to her. He was tall on the thin side, with a shadow of beard on his face and a stubble of crew-cut sand-brown hair on his head. He was wearing a grey sharkskin suit, a blue rep stripe tie, black shoes and dark blue socks. He was handsome without being obvious about it—the phrase that came to Saundra was *quiet good looks*. Now he was looking at her.

"Sit for a minute," Frank Ralston suggested. "It's a real mob scene. Ever since they stopped televising the fights, the Garden's been drawing heavily. Let's wait until the place clears out a little."

She decided that was a good idea. She looked for cigarettes in her purse but he beat her to the punch, shaking a cigarette loose from his pack and extending the pack to her. She took the proffered cigarette and put it to her lips, then accepted a light from him.

"It's a little better now," he was saying. "Let's go." They went.

The cab dropped them at the Showboard, a cocktail lounge on East 53rd Street. A very self-confident maître d' led them on a precarious journey through tightly packed tables to an empty table not far from the small stage. A piano looked lonely on the stage. No one was playing it.

The table they occupied was the size of a large postage stamp. Airmail, Saundra decided. They sat there, looking at each other, until a waiter arrived to take their drink order.

"Martini," Frank said crisply. "Extra dry, twist of lemon." He turned to Saundra. "Same for you, baby?"

Saundra nodded. She did not particularly like martinis, but she had the feeling that the waiter would smack his lips and shake his head if she ordered anything else. The Showboard was obviously a bar that catered to the complex of advertising, public relations and television. Martinis, extra dry with a twist, were the rule. She did not feel like breaking the rule.

"You look lovely tonight," Frank was telling her now. She accepted the compliment graciously, privately convinced that it was nothing more than the truth. She was wearing a simple green dress. She was a redhead, and green-eyed redheads had to work at it *not* to look good in simple green dresses. Her hair was done right, her face pretty, her body voluptuous as ever. Of course she looked lovely.

He ran his hand through his hair, a neat trick with a crew-cut, and smiled boyishly. "God above," he said, "I'm glad this week is over. It's been a bad one."

"Hard work?"

"Conferences," he said. "Brain trust sessions. Let's all get together and toss a few logs on the fire. Run it up the flagpole and see if anybody salutes. The same old cliches over and over. It's enough to give you a headache."

She nodded sympathetically.

The waiter came, bearing drinks. They sipped theirs—while the taste didn't exactly send Saundra into orbit, the drink was properly cold and properly crisp.

"If it's such a rut," she said, "why don't you quit?"

He grinned disarmingly. "I wondered when you'd get around to asking. A couple of reasons. For one thing, the work is challenging. It's not a case of insert-swoggle-A-into-bortsch-icle-B. It's a definite challenge."

"What's so challenging about persuading some house-wives that new blue Drear is better than Brand X?"

He laughed. "Good question. All right—so the main ob-jective is a lot of bull. Most things are. But once the rules are laid down, the rest is challenging. The procedures, the ploys in the game. You're touting new blue Drear. Some other joker is pushing Brand X. You've got to find a way to beat him out."

"I suppose so."

"You look doubtful. All right, there's more to it. For one thing, what the hell else is an English major supposed to do? Become a writer and starve to death? Get a teaching job in Backwater College and starve to death while dying of boredom? Hell, I make better than seven thou a year right now. And I'm just starting. A few more years and I'll be an account executive. Twenty grand a year, a house in Connecticut, a wife, two-point-seven-six children, an ulcer, a mistress and a psychoanalyst to support. That's a future."

Now she was laughing. He caught the waiter's eye and pointed to their glasses but she shook her head—her drink was still almost full. He told the waiter to make it just one for the time being.

He talked his way through the next drink, during which time the piano player, a goateed individual with a houndstooth sport jacket and suede shoes, put in his appearance. He played sophisticated mickey mouse piano and sang vulgar songs.

"Insecure world," Frank Ralston said. "H-Bomb like a Sword of Damocles. Pressure, pressure, pressure."

> *The queen was in the parlor*
> *Eating bread and honey*
> *The king was in the chambermaid*
> *And the maid was in the money . . .*

"Need for a goal," Frank Ralston said. "Helter-skelter sort of situation. Moral bankruptcy. Conformity."

Your father and your mother in yonder room do lie
Enjoying one another, so why not you and I?
Enjoying one another with ne'r a care or doubt
So roll me in your arms, love, and blow the candle out.

"Crazy, mixed up world," Frank Ralston said. "I think I'm getting a little bit fried. I think I'm getting a little sick of the Showboard. Anyplace you'd like to go?"

Saundra smiled. "We could go to your place," she suggested. "For a nightcap."

He looked surprised. "Isn't that supposed to be my line?"

"But I didn't think you were going to get around to it," she said. "Not for a while, anyway, and I don't feel like any more martinis or anything. So I decided to steal your line. Let's go up to your place for a nightcap."

"A fine idea," he said.

He called for the check, found a wallet and put money on the table. The waiter wished them both a good evening. Saundra liked that. She sincerely hoped that it would be a good evening. It had all the earmarks of one.

Outside the night was as cool and crisp as a martini, extra dry with a twist. Stars winked at them. There was no moon. She looked up at the sky and decided that it was appropriate. She was out with an ad man and the sky was charcoal grey.

"My place or yours?"

"Yours, Frank."

"Small," he said. "And ugly. Haven't had a chance to clean up for too long. You sure?"

"I have a roommate who stays home too often."

"My place, then."

They piled into a cab and Frank gave his address. The cab sped off into the night. She leaned a little against him. He tilted her face with one hand and kissed her expertly upon the mouth. A hand found her breast and squeezed reassuringly.

"A shame about your roommate," he breathed into her ear. "Staying home all alone. Nobody should have to be alone on a night like this one."

"She's a funny one," Saundra said.

"She must be."

YOU'RE A FUNNY one, Joan thought to herself.

She was alone in the apartment. Earlier she had been sitting in the living room. Now, however, it was after twelve o'clock. At twelve o'clock on the dot she had closed her book and carried it into her bedroom. Now she was lying on the bed, shoes off, propped up on her elbows, the book resting on the bed in front of her. The book was a thin volume, a collection of verse by a young poet named Cornwall Becke. Joan was reading a poem entitled "Johnny Appleseed."

> *Brave and bent and bleak*
> *as the last poplar on a northern peak*
> *I walk alone—*
> *on a road that winds forever*
> *with my skin like shrunken leather*

drying tautly on the bone.
My road will always wind uphill
and I shall always carry in my back
a million tomorrows in a gunny sack
the hungry sperm cells of a cider mill . . .

She shifted position slightly, trying to get comfortable. She had been very comfortable in the big soft chair in the living room. But, in line with Marilyn's request, she had vacated that room precisely on the stroke of twelve. Marilyn had been quite explicit.

"I'll be bringing a man up," she had said. "Between twelve and one. I'd rather you weren't in the living room just then, sweets. It can get awkward, stopping to chat and trying to be nonchalant while we waltz into my bedroom. So if you could manage to find your way to your own room at twelve, say, and stay there until we get to my bedroom, well, I'd appreciate it. Then you can go back, I mean, once we're in there. If he sees you on the way out it won't make any difference. Or if he's there in the morning. We can all have breakfast together. It'll be cozy."

"Who's the man? "

"I don't know," Marilyn had answered, combining a shrug with a smile. "I haven't picked him out yet."

Breakfast together, Joan thought. Cozy.

She read the poem over. It was not a hard poem to follow but she was having trouble concentrating. Memories of the night before kept intruding. Memories of Terri, and Terri's good body, and what the two of them had done. She remembered holding Terri in her arms after it was over.

Tomorrows always come
and poplars always fall;
Yesterday was heaven, after all—
Why should tomorrow be?

Now she was alone. Alone through choice, in a strange but true way. The loneliness of her life was self-chosen. She could live like Terri—an apartment in the Village, the companionship of other lesbians. She could shack up with another girl, let her own aberrations become public knowledge, accept herself and admit herself to the world. She did not do this.

She was a lesbian. But the people who knew Joan McKay did not know that she was a lesbian, and the girls who knew what she was did not know *who* she was. She lived in two worlds. One of them was divided between the apartment on East 73rd Street and the *Agony* office. The other existed in lesbian bars and lesbian beds.

She wondered why. Maybe she couldn't entirely accept what she was. Maybe she was afraid of herself, afraid of the world, afraid of what she was. Maybe she wanted to be . . . normal.

I do not want to die.

I will not see
My name reduced to writing on the sky;
Worms in my body, bugs upon my face.
Nor will I rest as ashes in a vase,
a note of everybody's doom
in someone's jaded living room
over the fireplace.

Then she heard it. A door opening, the door of the apartment, no doubt, the door opened by Marilyn. She heard Marilyn's voice, little more than a whisper, and she heard another lower voice. A man. The man who would be making violent love to Marilyn in just a few minutes. The man who would push his harshness into her softness, the man who would fill her with himself and make her cry out.

She heard their footsteps in the living room, heard ice cubes swirling in two glasses, heard liquor gurgling over the cubes of ice. She heard glasses clink together. She heard more whispering, and then she heard silence, and she tried to concentrate on the poem. She did not want to think about what she could hear. Nor did she want to think about what she could not hear.

I will not die. No, I will not be bound
By urn or box but planted in the ground
and from my toes and fingers trees shall grow
straight, strong and tall, reaching to tie

the sinking earth against the floating sky.
And when my steel bones rot
they'll turn to wood that's twice as strong and joins
then to again, bearing fruit flesh-fresh, the hot
eternal offspring of forgotten loins.
And while ten thousand corpses wonder why,
I shall not die.

The poem was an affirmation. A song to immortality. A reason for planting trees, a reason for writing poems, a reason for leaving something on earth behind you.

A reason for children.

But lesbians did not have children. Lesbians died, and when they were dead it was as though they had never been in the first place. They left the world and the world was no emptier without them. They disappeared and left no traces.

She closed the book.

Footsteps, again. Footsteps moving from the living room to the bedroom. Not to her bedroom, but to Marilyn's bedroom. A door creaking open—they had to buy some oil, go over the hinges. It was a pain in the neck the way the doors squeaked. The door squealing shut.

A moment's silence.

Joan's mind made pictures. She saw Marilyn in the arms of a man without a face, a lover lacking form or identity. She saw a man's hands on Marilyn's sweet breasts, a man's hand removing Marilyn's clothing, a man's mouth kissing Marilyn and the maleness of a man profaning that body.

God.

There had to be a way to turn her mind off. It was bad, very bad, and the little sounds that came from Marilyn's room were no help at all. Only a thin wall separated the two bedrooms. A thin wall. And while she could not hear enough to know what was happening, she could hear enough to imagine. And imagination, in this case, was worse than knowledge. Imagination that generated desire of its own. Desire that could lead only to frustration, and frustration that could do nothing but make matters worse. As if they were not bad enough as they were.

God.

What were they doing now? And who was the man, and what did he look like, and where had she found him?

And why? Why did she have to go and pick up a man, a miserable damned man? Why?

I deserve this, she thought. I honest to God deserve it. How dumb can I be? A brilliant type. A dyed-in-the-wool dyke living with a pair of beautiful lovely gorgeous girls who wear out two mattresses a week. Two nymphs and a dyke.

A man on a diet living across the street from a candy factory.

God!

"GOD!"

Marilyn's voice was a whisper. Just a whisper, but a forceful one. That single syllable summed up a lot of things. They way she felt, for example.

She felt magnificent.

The man's name, if he was to be believed, was Joe. He was an outlander from Kansas City, but he was not the typical visiting fireman. An intelligent man, a man with poise. And no fat fool with a paunch. Mid-thirties, she guessed. Vibrant and gutsy and hard-muscled. Alive.

One of them had picked up the other in the Astor Bar. It was a moot point as to who had done the up-picking. He thought he did, and that was fine with her. Let him feel good. She certainly didn't care who had been the aggressor in their little old relationship. They were together now, and they would be together for the entire night, and that was as much as she cared about. Let him go back to Kansas City and brag about his conquests. She didn't really care. She was having her fun.

She was naked. He still wore his undershorts, but soon they would be off and the two of them would be able to get down to brass tacks. In the meantime, until they hit brass tacks, they were doing fine. She was lying flat on her back on the bed, her head resting comfortably on the foam rubber pillow, and he was fooling around with her breasts.

She enjoyed this. She had been blessed with extremely nice breasts. His hands did nice things to them. She reached out and ran her fingers across his chest.

The right way to finish the damned week. The only way. Work done, get the hell out of the office, a drink at Michael's Pub, a solitary dinner at the best steakhouse in midtown Manhattan. A blood-rare sirloin and a big baked potato, a crisp salad with Roquefort, a pony of cognac afterwards. Then a Broadway show, alone again, a good funny one so that she could just relax and enjoy it, nothing deep, nothing that would make her think. Not after five days at Phulcorte, not after five brain-breaking days. No more thinking, not until the weekend was over and the grind began again.

And, after the show, a drink at the Astor Bar. He was not hard to find. He was a man looking for a girl to pick up, and she was a girl looking for a man to pick up, and that was that. She took out a cigarette and glanced around vacantly for a match. He supplied the match. She thanked him and gave him a smile that was neither too hot nor too cold. He bought the next round of drinks.

From there it was a short distance to the bedroom. The shortest distance is a straight line. That was more or less the course that they had taken.

Now they arrived.

He was lying down beside her now, taking her in his arms. He held her close and her body shivered with pleasure at the contact. This was the way, she thought. The only sensible way. Find what you want and get hold of it. Find the right man, the right man for the evening, and spend the evening with him. Do what you want to do, what you have to do. Get the pleasure you need. Go tense and then relax again.

The only way.

He kissed her and his tongue entered her mouth. His tongue tasted of tobacco and bonded bourbon. That, he had informed her, was all a man drank in Kay Cee. Like a martini on Ulcer Gulch or Sneaky Pete on the Bowery. He had laughed when he said it. He had a good laugh.

He also had a wife, unless she missed her guess. This did not bother her. She was not a woman in love but a woman in heat. She did not care if he had seven wives, just so long as they were not in the same room with her.

Now he was caressing her body, his hands warm and sure on her. He had touched her in the taxi. Then, of course, she had had clothes on. But it was better now. Much better.

He caressed her and her body sang out.

Two could play that game. Her hand, as clever as his, reached for him.

He laughed—an eminently earthy laugh. He touched himself to her and her body quivered.

"Now?"

"Now."

Now it was. This was it, the ball game, the brass tacks reached at last. This was what mattered, all that mattered, this was what all the shouting was about.

The two of them.

Together.

She breathed in deeply and her breasts were flat against his chest.

She hugged her arms tight around him and squeezed. Each movement sent a new thrill of pleasure through her.

He was an expert.

Her hands reached down, holding him tight, close to her, with her. He moved again, magnificently, and she began to twist like a serpent.

It always got like this. This, perhaps, was the big thing about love for her. It got too big for her. It got so big that her mind didn't work anymore. Her mind turned off and there was only her body, a body with a will all its own. She couldn't tell her body what to do, not once it got going. She could only act without any volition.

This happened now.

There was his body and there was her body and that was all there was. There was Him, and there was Her, receiving him.

Nothing more.

The bed sprouted wings and sailed away. The walls disappeared and the world flattened out and dissolved. They were alone, wheels within wheels in the middle of the air.

Her hands raked his back. Her teeth bit into his shoulder. Her legs tightened into bands of steel and her heart pounded much faster than any heart was supposed to pound.

Just the two of them.

And then it was happening, the only thing that counted, the only thing in all the world that makes everything right. The only thing that soothed the hurts and levelled the depressions and made life worth living. It was happening; happening to her and for her, happening now, now, now.

And with a shake and a shudder and a sigh and a moan they were there, there, there, and the world was good.

AND THEN IT was happening, the only thing that counted, the only thing in all the world that made everything right. The only thing that soothed the hurts and levelled the depressions and made life worth living. It was happening; happening to her and for her; happening now, now, now.

And with a shake and a shudder and a sigh and a moan they were there, there, there, and the world was good.

Frank was the first to move. Saundra lay very still, secure in a blanket of sweetness, and knew he was moving away from her. She did not open her eyes. She did not move.

"You're wonderful," he said.

She mumbled something unintelligible.

"Wonderful. Like no other girl I've ever met in my life. I needed you, Sandstone. You have no idea how much I needed you. I couldn't possibly explain it to you."

She did not say anything.

"Was it good for you, baby?"

"Uh-huh."

"I'm glad. I wanted it to be good for you, baby. We work out all right together, you know. A team."

She had a fairly good idea what he was getting at. If she was right, the conversation was heading toward dangerous ground. She hoped he would stop. She wanted to have him lie down beside her, to close his eyes and his mouth, and to warm her body with his own. The aftermath was far too pleasant to be marred by conversation. Especially the sort of conversation he was steering toward.

She wished he would stop.

He didn't.

"Good together," he repeated. "Not just in bed. That, of course, but it's not the only thing. Out of bed, we're still good. Talking, sitting around, having a drink, going to the fights. I feel a hell of a lot better when I'm with you, baby."

One date, and he was talking lines out of Romeo, by Tristan. Dumb jerk.

"I really like you," he went on, indefatigably. "As a person, I mean. This isn't just a . . . a quickie for me. That's not how I feel about you. I want something more than that. A . . . a full relationship. Maybe this sounds corny—"

It did.

"—but I have a lot of feelings for you. I don't want to rush things, baby. But sometimes—in this kind of a fast-moving world things can happen very quickly. This is a hell of a world. You know that. And we're not the general run of people. We're special And . . . you know what I'm getting at."

She knew what he was getting at.

And, evidently, it was not enough to ignore him. Frank Ralston took that sort of treatment as an encouraging sign. She lay quiet and said nary a word and it only served to build up his confidence. In another damned minute he was going to propose marriage, and if there was one thing on God's earth which did not interest her it was marriage to Frank Ralston.

Oh, he was a nice guy.

But the world was filled to overflowing with nice guys.

Oh, he was good in bed.

But the world was overflowing with guys who were good in bed, and some of them were better than Frank Ralston.

By his own admission, he worked like a Turk to make "better than seven thou a year." This she should marry?

No. This she should not marry.

She sat up suddenly, eyes open and blinking at the light, breasts rampant. She turned to look at him and searched her mind for a polite and tactful and gentle way to lower the boom.

"Frank," she said, "I don't want to get . . . serious or anything."

He blinked.

"I know you wouldn't even consider anything like marriage with me," she lied, "but I want to, well, lay it on the line before either of us gets carried away by what just happened. I'm not the marrying type, Frank. Not that I think you want to marry me, or would ever want to marry me. I just want to make sure you never feel, well, romantically obligated or anything. We're good together and that's good and I like it. So do you. But I just wanted to, well, make it plain."

If she made anything plain, she would be damned if she knew what it was. Her words, as far as she could determine, were double-talk. But they had a certain effect. The message was simply that they had a good thing going and they would continue to knock off one now and then with no strings on either side. That much could not fail to penetrate painlessly to his not-too-keen brain.

He nodded, thoughtfully, and then he smiled. His smile looked a little forced to her. Not too much. Just a little.

"Well," he said.

"Frank—" It was time to change the subject.

"What, baby?"

"I want you, Frank."

An open-eyed stare.

"I want you. Now."

"Well—"

Her hands touched his chest, his stomach.

"Let's," she cooed. "Let's again."

JOAN TOSSED IN her bed, unable to sleep. Marilyn and the nameless faceless man were at it again, having another go. This made the third time. It was torture. Sheer torture.

She heard the rhythmic sound of bedsprings and her mind was flooded once again with pictures. She couldn't take much more of this. If they didn't stop soon she was going to go out of her alleged mind.

Creak.

Her own hands cupped her breasts. Whose were they? Hers? Or Terri's, or Saundra's, or Marilyn's?

What did it matter?

Her hands roamed her body freely. She could not help herself.

Surely but shamefully she caressed herself to solitary fulfillment.

Chapter Four

MORNING, UNLIKE THE end of the world, comes with neither bang nor whimper. It comes most frequently with a sort of a dry belch. Morning is never particularly good. It varies only in degrees of objectionableness. There are bad mornings and there are worse mornings. The argument is not without merit that the bearableness of any given morning runs in inverse proportion to the pleasure of the night preceding that morning. When the night before is a gasser, the morning after is generally a dog.

Last night had been a good one. And the morning that followed it, Marilyn was not astounded to discover, was close to horrible. She opened one eye experimentally. Her head ached dully, her mouth tasted like an abandoned cesspool, her muscles hurt from too much delightful exercise.

She closed the eye.

She remembered the night, and she remembered Joe, and she said a silent prayer that he had awakened before her, had dressed, and was now gone. It was not that she did not like Joe, certainly not that she had not enjoyed his company. But, just as certain evenings are meant to be shared with others, certain mornings are meant to be spent in something approaching solitary confinement. This was one of them. She wanted to be alone, and if Joe was gone she would be happy.

Painfully she raised her head, turned it around, and propped her eyes open. He was not gone. He was still sharing her bed, his body only a few inches from her, flat on his back with his mouth slightly open and his eyes firmly shut. He was sleeping the sleep of the just, or of the dead, and Marilyn Harper was envious.

It took her a few minutes of concentrated struggle to get up from the warmth of the bed. She managed it, hoisted herself up onto tired legs and wandered over to the window. The sun was shining in a clear sky and it looked like a warm day. She wished she could appreciate the beauty of nature but somehow she wasn't quite up to it.

The bathroom was gratifyingly empty. She turned on the shower full blast and got under it. It made a considerable difference. She massaged the soap into her skin and worked up a rich lather that cleansed away the stains of passion that covered her body. She let the water lash at her in a fine spray that planted a thousand tiny needles in her flesh. She stepped out of the stall and wrapped herself in a huge bath towel, rubbing herself dry and pink.

This was the way she started every day. It was the only way she could get herself going, the only way to wash away the residue of the past day, mental and physical, and get started on something fresh and new.

Then she brushed her teeth four times. She was back in her bedroom, half dressed in skirt and blouse, when his eyes opened.

"Hello," he said.

"Don't try to talk until after you shower," she told him. "I just got up. I know how your head feels. The bathroom's down the hall to your right. I left a towel out for you. Lots of luck."

When he had finished his shower and was dressed, she had the beginnings of breakfast on the table. The stereotype of the career girl is lost in the kitchen. While Marilyn may have fitted the mold in other respects, here she deviated from form. She was not a wizard with pots and pans, not an artist-in-apron, but she was competent. The table was set for three (she knew damned well that Sandstone hadn't come home the night before) with plates and silverware and glasses of cold orange juice. He sat down opposite her, looking clean and crisp and not nearly so awkward or uncomfortable as she had expected, and raised his glass in a mock toast.

"To morning," he said.

"May it pass quickly," she replied. They tossed off their glasses of juice like shots of vodka at a Russian dinner party. Then she stood up.

"How do you like your coffee?"

"Hot, black, no sugar, and now."

She grinned. The coffee was ready; the noisy electric percolator had quieted down. She put two cups on the table and filled them to the brim. Then she picked up the plates and filled them with scrambled eggs and chicken livers.

"This," he said, "is a meal."

"Everything okay?"

"Delicious. I didn't know you could cook, too."

"You picked up a bargain."

He smiled.

They passed the rest of the meal in relative silence. The small talk they made was very small. He lit a cigarette to go with his second cup of coffee and gave her one, lighting it for her. She drew smoke into her lungs, blew it out, sipped her coffee. Only then did she feel entirely awake.

Now she looked across the table at him. He needed a shave, of course. And his shirt was a little rumpled. But otherwise he looked unbelievably good. His straight black hair was combed neatly and his skin was pink and alive. His eyes were alert, attentive. He sat straight in his chair, a good-looking man about thirty-five, with whom she had spent the night.

"What time is it?" he asked suddenly.

"A little after eleven. Why?"

"I've got a business appointment at one-thirty."

"You'd better get going," she suggested. "You'll want to stop at your hotel before the appointment to change your clothes."

"I've got a few minutes."

She didn't say anything.

"About tonight," he said. "Will you have dinner with me tonight? Then we can catch a show. I don't have tickets, but it shouldn't be too hard to pick up a decent pair."

Her mouth nearly fell open. This was a little too much—what was he trying to do, make a regular job of it? Why not move out of his hotel and park his bags in her bedroom?

"Marilyn?"

She set her jaw. "I'm afraid not," she said.

He looked surprised.

"Your wife will miss you," she said. "I wouldn't want to keep you from her. But if you're anxious, just hit the Astor Bar again. Some other girl'll turn up. You won't have to sleep alone."

"My wife?"

"You're married, Joe. Don't give me that."

"I *was* married. Happily married, as a matter of fact. But Janice died two years ago."

She was stunned. She lowered her eyes and for a moment she said nothing.

"I guess I stepped in my mouth," she said finally. "I have a talent for that sort of thing. I'm sorry, Joe."

"It was a natural mistake."

"I only thought—"

"I know what you thought. Let's forget about it. Will you have dinner with me?"

"If the invitation still holds."

"It holds."

"Then I'd like to have dinner with you, Joe." She smiled, her face relaxing. "I'd like that very much."

*   *   *

SAUNDRA STONE, IN contradiction of Marilyn's theory, *was* in her own bedroom. She arrived there at approximately four o'clock in the morning. After a second bout with Frank Ralston, her intrepid lover had quickly dropped off to a deep sleep. Sandstone would have loved to join him. But she knew better. If there was one place she didn't want to be, it was his apartment when he awoke the next morning. And she couldn't trust herself to wake up before him. She was too sound a sleeper. So, much as she would have loved to curl up and close her eyes, she had forced herself to dress and leave Frank's bachelor apartment on West 69th Street and catch a cab crosstown to her own place.

Now it was morning and she was awake. She listened to voices in the kitchen, one male voice and one female voice, and identified the latter as Marilyn's and the former as an unknown. A peek in the mirror convinced herself that it would be best to remain in her bedroom until the unknown left rather than risk scaring him half to death. She looked, speaking plainly, like hell.

Finally each of the two voices said goodbye to the other voice and Saundra heard a door slam. She counted to twenty by tens, then opened the door and looked out. Marilyn was standing deep in thought in the middle of the living room.

"Hello," she said.

Marilyn stared. "What are you doing here?"

"I live here. Remember?"

"I thought you were going to get banged."

"I *did*," Saundra explained. "Then I came home. In that order."

"But—"

"You reversed the order. You came home and then you got banged. It takes all kinds. How was he?"

"Fine, but—"

"I had to clear out," Sandstone explained again. "I was with Frank at his apartment. He brought up an unpleasant subject. Started to anyway."

"What subject?"

"Marriage."

"Ughhhhh."

"So I left."

"But you did get—"

"Resoundingly."

"Oh."

"And to hell with you," Sandstone went on. "For the time being, anyway. I need a shower. Later we'll talk."

Saundra Stone was not the breakfast type. After her shower she sat in the living room with as much breakfast as she could ever tolerate, a single cup of black coffee. She drank it slowly.

"Tonight," she said. "Tonight it's hunting time. Tonight I have a date with a rich man."

"Who?"

"Johnny Lipton."

Marilyn whistled softly.

"The brokerage Liptons," Saundra said, needlessly. "Also the iron-and-steel Liptons, and the chemical Liptons. Johnny is rich. Stinking rich is, I think, the proper term. Or filthy rich. Rich, no matter how you look at it."

"And you want to marry him."

"Who wouldn't?"

Marilyn grinned. "What's on the agenda for tonight?"

"Dinner at Marmaduke's," Saundra intoned, rolling her eyes dreamily. "Drinks somewhere properly exclusive. And then a party."

"What kind of party?"

"I have an idea."

Marilyn waited.

"I think," Sandstone said, "it's going to be an orgy."

"Huh!"

"Not exactly," Saundra said. "I've got that wrong. Let me start over. There are a couple of places in this here town where just about anything goes. There's one specifically that Johnny mentioned. It's a nightclub, more or less, except that it is not easy to get past the door and except that the floorshow is rather way out."

"Like?"

"Like sex on stage."

"A hot strip show?"

"Nope."

"Then—"

"Like a stag movie," Saundra said. "Except not a movie. Live. On stage. In living color."

"Oh."

"Is that all you can say?"

"Uh-huh. That's about it."

"It should be fun," Saundra said. "I've never been to any-thing like that before. I saw a movie once. Ever see one of those?"

"Nope."

"Interesting. But it was in black-and-white, and it was an old print spliced to hell and back, and the girl was homely as sin. Homelier. Come to think about it, sin isn't homely. It's beautiful."

IT WAS AFTERNOON. Three in the afternoon, give or take a few minutes. There was never any way to be sure just what time it was when you had a watch like Joan McKay's. It was a compulsive liar, that watch. Always a little bit wrong.

Joan was in the *Agony* office. The *Agony* office was a cubicle on the fourth floor of a four-story brick building on University Place between Thirteenth and Fourteenth Streets. Neither office nor building was calculated to impress anybody. It had, however, impressed the daylights out of Joan the first time she had set eyes on it, reporting for work to Harvey Chase. Then it had symbolized Art and Literature and Hopes and Dreams.

Now she saw it with the rose-colored spectacles stowed away somewhere. Now it was a run-down room with run-down furniture. But it was still a refuge. She was genuinely comfortable in the small office, so much so that she was spending her time there on a Saturday afternoon, the only person in the office, working on her own time.

But there was work to do, and there was certainly nothing *else* to do. A whole stack of brown manila envelopes containing unknown and generally unwanted manuscripts from unknown and generally unwanted authors waited for her attention. She had to separate wheat from chaff. There was still a little room in the September issue—Harvey could use a poem or two, possibly a story if she could come up with something good.

She sighed. Then she picked up the long silver letter-knife and opened the first envelope.

The title was *As the Twig is Bent* and the author was someone named Mabel Whitcomb Lewis. Joan could have stopped right there. At least three times a week a script came into the *Agony* office entitled *As the Twig is Bent*. The author was invariably a woman with three names. And the script was invariably lousy.

The present case proved no exception. It took only one paragraph of Mabel Whitcomb Lewis's tortuous prose to assure Joan that Mabel was incapable of writing English. The woman, bless her, approached the English language like a bomb approaching a target. She exploded all over the page and the results were nauseating.

Dutifully Joan transcribed Mabel Whitcomb Lewis's name and address on a 3x5 index card. Now and forevermore Mabel Whitcomb Lewis would be invited to subscribe to *Ag-*

ony, to give Christmas presents of *Agony* subscriptions, to buy books from *Agony*, and to support the cause of literature and art, by donating money to *Agony*.

Then Joan placed Mabel Whitcomb Lewis's horrible story into the return envelope which Mabel Whitcomb Lewis had thoughtfully provided, took a printed rejection slip from her desk drawer, scrawled *sorry* on it in pencil, and put it in the envelope with the script. Authors always drooled all over the place when they got a hand-written *sorry* on the rejection slip. They thought it meant something. It didn't.

Not that Joan *wasn't* sorry. She was. Heartily sorry that Mabel Whitcomb Lewis didn't knit or garden or play with herself. Anything at all, just so she didn't write.

The next few scripts were not much better. On two she stopped before the end of the first page. Then there were two more which she read all the way through before rejecting. Then a poem, truly free verse, lacking not only rhyme but reason as well. Then a batch of poems that were fairly good—she placed these in Harvey Chase's IN basket. He might like them. She didn't, not especially, but he might. Then again, he might not.

The next envelope was the killer.

On the outside it looked like any other envelope. Nine inches by twelve inches, brown manila paper. A clasp securing the flap. Stamps in the upper-right-hand corner. A FIRST CLASS MAIL DO NOT BEND sticker. *Agony's* address, painfully handprinted. No return address, but that was not too unusual.

She opened the envelope.

Two sheets of cardboard protected the envelope's contents. The contents were not at all the normal run. There was only a single sheet of white bond paper. On both sides of it the same single word was typed again and again and again.

It was a four-letter word and it rhymed with *luck*.

When the same word appears a few hundred times on a page, it loses its significance. No longer does it have any meaning at all. It's a combination of meaningless letters, and it looks wrong, and it's silly.

Consider the word *camp*. A simple, ordinary word. But look at this:

camp camp camp camp camp camp

camp camp camp camp camp

camp camp camp camp camp camp

camp camp camp camp camp

Well, that's enough. You get the general idea. That's what confronted Joan, only the word was not *camp*. It was something else entirely.

She stared at the single sheet of paper in fascination, a morbid sort of fascination. She tried to figure out what manner of idiot would send such a sheet of paper to *Agony*. A person would have to be pretty well demented to expect *Agony* to publish his little poem, or story, or whatever it was supposed to be.

She put the paper down.

And noticed the rest.

The photographs.

The anonymous contributor, whoever he might be, was obviously a nut. For reasons known only to himself and God, and perhaps only to God, he had sent a sheaf of totally vulgar photographs to *Agony*. The pictures were all eight-by-eleven black and white glossies, perfectly exposed, probably professional work. The contents of the pictures were alarming.

At first Joan merely stared at the top picture, a sweet little shot of a man lying on his back with a woman on top of him, straddling him. She stared for an indefinable length of time. Then, numbly, her hands shuffled through the stack of photographs and considered each in turn.

There were an even dozen. They were all variations on the same theme, of course. That much should go without saying. But some of the variations were incredibly varied.

Very varied.

In one shot a wild-eyed girl stood in the middle of the floor wearing nothing but an expression of hysterical glee while two men embraced her, one from the front and the other from the rear. The picture was a side view and revealed to the camera and to the world what they were doing.

In another shot the girl filled the one cavity of her body which hadn't come into play before. Naturally, in the interests of greater detail, only her head appeared in this picture.

These pictures were bad. Very bad. And, looking at them, Joan felt herself beginning to tremble. Her hands were steady, her forehead cool. The trembling was going on inside. It was infinitely worse that way.

The worst was yet to come. The worst *did* come when she hit the final picture. It was a little different from the others. In this picture there were two girls and a man. One of the girls was blonde, the other a brunette. It made for good photographic contrast, Joan thought.

The blonde was lying on her back. Her thighs, golden and full, were parted. A man was with her.

This did not particularly bother Joan.

It was the other girl who bothered Joan. The other girl, the brunette, was crouched over the blonde in such a way that the blonde was doing something to the other girl. It was quite a picture.

It had quite an effect.

Joan McKay began to sweat. She looked at the blonde, and she looked at the brunette, and she saw what the blonde was doing and her heart skipped a beat. As far as she was concerned the man might just as well have been snipped from the picture. The only thing that mattered was what the blonde was doing to the brunette. Nothing else was important.

It took her a long time before she was able to relax. She'd planned on a quiet evening that night. A movie—there was a good foreign import uptown at the Thalia. A quiet walk in the warm air, then a bus back to the apartment and a few hours of auto-hypnosis in front of the one-eyed monster, the television set.

Now her plans were shot to hell.

Because it was not going to be that sort of night at all. She had been relaxed after that night with Terri, all loose and calm and collected. Then, in quick succession, she had been treated to the squealing springs of Marilyn's mattress and now this, a vulgar parcel that was foul and, damn it to hell, emotionally disturbing.

She picked up the envelope, looked at the postmark. It had occurred to her that perhaps someone had sent this to her deliberately. One of the girls could have done it, for example. It might be Sandstone's brilliant idea to throw a little life into the Vestal Virgin.

But the postmark was Chicago. She did not know anybody in Chicago. And it seemed highly unlikely that Sandstone would go to Chicago just to mail Joan some vulgar pictures.

Maybe they were for Harvey. It seemed insane, but he might have ordered them for some perverse reason all his own. Lots of men liked to look at such pictures, according to what she had heard. Harvey Chase hardly seemed the type, but then you never knew.

But would he order them sent to the magazine?

She quit thinking and dialed his home number.

He answered the phone, his voice sounding a little drunk, which was usually the case with Harvey Chase. When the week ended, he drank. It was his privilege, she thought.

"Joan, Harvey," she said. "Look, this is going to sound silly. Did you order any pictures?"

"Huh?"

"Let me start at the beginning. I'm at the office, Harvey. I came in and—"

"You didn't have to."

"I know, but I had nothing else to do. Anyway, I was going through the slush—"

"Anything good?"

"A few poems. Short stuff, meaty, terse. A little like the stuff Josephine Miles writes. Mostly eight-liners, one or two twelves. I think you might like them."

"Do you like them?"

"Not especially."

"Well, I'll take a look at them. Did you say something about pictures?"

"I was trying to. In one of the envelopes, Harvey. Addressed to *Agony*, a regular manila envelope mailed in Chicago and filled with a dozen pictures. They're . . . they're filthy. You know—vulgar pictures."

"Nudes?"

"Shots of couples engaging in sexual intercourse, to be clinical. You know what I mean."

He whistled softly. When you whistle into the mouthpiece of a telephone you evidence little concern for the person on the other end of the line. Joan winced and rubbed her ear.

"Did you order them, Harvey?"

"Hell, no. What would *I* want with them?"

"I don't know."

"If I want to watch two people making love," Harvey said, "I get myself a girl and a mirror, prop up one in front of the other, and watch *myself*. Not two total strangers. What kind of a nut do you think I am?"

"Well—"

"Chuck 'em out," he said. "I don't even want to see 'em. Burn 'em, rip 'em, or keep 'em and paste 'em on your walls. I don't care."

"But—"

"Just leave me out of it," he went on. "It's only Saturday. I mean it's Saturday, almost four-thirty, and I have a lot of serious drinking to do. People like you can afford to work on a Saturday. I can't. I have a whole fifth to get through by nightfall, and I'm way behind schedule. Goodbye."

And he hung up on her.

She sat there for a moment or two with the receiver in her hand, thinking that Harvey Chase was an unusual man indeed. The pictures, evidently, were hers to do with what she would. Accordingly she did what to her seemed to be the only conceivable thing. She shredded them until they were totally undistinguishable from pictures of a picnic in the park. And she threw them into the wastebasket.

But they had already had their effect.

It would not be a quiet evening alone. Not now, not after what that damned blonde had been doing to that equally damned brunette. It would be an unquiet evening with another girl. Another girl like Terri.

She did not want it to happen. But it was going to, damn it, and there was nothing she could possibly do about it. When you had an itch you scratched. Period.

It would be nice to be normal, Joan thought. It would be pleasant if her itches were the same as those of Saundra and Marilyn, if the same sort of activity would scratch hers as scratched theirs. Her appetite was no greater than theirs, her hungers no more intense. She needed sex and so did they. They needed it and they took what they needed, and they were proud of themselves, proud that they were free women with modern morals and a solid understanding of their desires and needs.

Yet she alone had to live in secret. Her passion was private—her roommates could not know of it and her lovers could not know her own name. Her desires were so evil, so perverted in the eyes of the world—and, perhaps, in her own eyes as well—that she had to pretend frigidity instead. No desires at all were more acceptable to the world than forbidden desires. Sexlessness was to be preferred to the curse word of lesbianism.

Now sweat was gluing her blouse to her body. She had not worn a bra that day and she looked down at her breasts, outlined against the white cloth. She remembered the breasts of the blonde girl in the picture. She remembered what the blonde girl had been doing. And she thought that she, too, was a blonde. And that she too, would be doing the very same thing that night.

She left the office and locked the door behind her. She walked down three ill-lit flights of stairs to the street below. The sun had vanished behind clouds but the air was still warm, June-warm.

She was on Fourteenth Street now, the northernmost edge of the Village. She could grab a meal in an Italian restaurant, then find a gay bar and make a pick-up. But that did not appeal this evening. The Village was a pain in the neck. She wanted to go to a gay bar, but not the loud and lousy downtown variety. Something uptown, something cool.

The blouse and slacks she wore would not do. She had to get home and change, have a meal somewhere, then go out on the town dressed to fracture if not kill. Find the right club, the moving club, the gently and jubilant gay club. A place where the drinks were a dollar and a quarter apiece and the company was fast and loose.

She walked to the East Side IRT, went down a flight of cold stone steps and bought a token from the Negro woman in the change booth. She dropped the small brass check in the slot and passed through the turnstile. The platform was almost empty and there was room for her to sit down on the hard bench.

Chapter Five

JOHNNY LIPTON LOOKED depraved.

The point is that Johnny Lipton didn't just *look* depraved. He *was* depraved.

Sandstone had never slept with Johnny Lipton, but she knew this. She had never so much as kissed him, yet she still knew this for a fact. She looked at him and a smile moved into place on her lips. Depraved or not, he was a good looking guy. Wavy black hair, every strand in place. High cheekbones, a narrow nose. Strictly aristocratic features, inherited no doubt from his great-grandfather, a man named Hezekiah Abner Lipton. Old H. A. had founded an aristocratic line by the simple expedient of robbing the country blind, slitting his competitors' throats with a rusty razor, milking and mulcting the public, and otherwise making a genuine louse of himself.

They were seated across a tiny marble-topped table by the window in Peak of the Plaza, a cocktail lounge located on the top floor of the Deekman-Plaza Hotel. The window looked out at the East River, and the terrace surrounding the lounge afforded a star-covered view of the area, starting with the impressive United Nations building and winding up with a Pepsi-Cola sign in winking red neon. She was sipping a frozen daiquiri while he worked on a bourbon sour. Smoke trailed to the ceiling from two cigarettes resting side by side in the heavy ashtray.

She smiled her approval, trying to fit herself into the perfect mood for the evening. It was going to be touchy—her object, of course, was to wind up labelled Mrs. Johnny Lipton, and such an aim would be a difficult one to achieve. Playing hard to get bed-wise would not work with Johnny. Some men married a girl if there was no other way to get under her skirt, but Johnny wasn't that type of man. The world was full to overflowing with girls more than willing to delight him. If a girl held out, he said to hell with her forever and looked elsewhere. So the hard-to-get approach was out.

So, she thought, was the old ploy of making the man fall in love with her. Johnny just wasn't the let's-fall-in-love type. She was relatively certain he had never loved anyone in his life with the possible exception of himself. And he probably *never* would love anyone else. Even if he married her, he would not love her. It wouldn't work that way.

What ploys were left?

There was only one that made any sense to her. That was simply one of being the perfect companion for Johnny. If she could prove herself one-hundred percent satisfactory in cocktail lounge, across dinner table, in company, and in the hay then things might well break right for her. Johnny wouldn't love her, but he might decide he wanted to have her around on a permanent basis. You do not have to love an automobile to buy it. You just have to feel that it's the car you want to own.

I'll be a fine car, she thought, grinning inwardly. I'll give him a ride he'll never forget.

"Another drink?" he was saying. "Or should we go get something to eat now?"

She put her hand over the mouth of her glass. "No more for me right now. But have another if you want."

He shook his head, motioned for the waiter, dropped money for the tip on the table and scrawled his name on the bar check. Then they were leaving the Peak of the Plaza, plummeting groundward in the elevator, landing on the street and getting into a cab thoughtfully hailed by the uniformed doorman.

The restaurant was located on East Sixty-Fourth Street between Second and Third Avenues. Few restaurants in the world were less ostentatious or more exclusive. Marmaduke's never advertised. Marmaduke's, in fact, did not even have a sign in front to tell the outside world where it was. A tall man with a pencil-line moustache and wearing a tuxedo stood on the doorstep of a plushy remodeled brownstone. He seemed to be relaxing, taking air. When Johnny gave his name he did not have to check a guest list. He was paid to remember names.

The doorman passed them through and the maître d' picked them up, leading them through the main dining room to an antechamber with two small tables in it. Saundra and Johnny took one table. The other was already occupied, and

Saundra recognized the couple. The woman was a famous Hollywood actress a year or two or three past her prime. The man with her was younger, and Sandstone guessed he was working for a living, working as the actress's lover. It did not look like hard work. The actress was still very beautiful. Most men would have made love to her with no remuneration.

The entire restaurant was done in sumptuous colonial styling—massive hewn oak beams on the ceilings, thick carpeting underfoot, portraits on the walls, elaborate candelabra, and all the little joys of life that made the manor house different from the log cabin.

The food was phenomenal.

The waiter took care of ordering the meal, this at Johnny's suggestion. "They're very fine here," he explained. "At too many places, if you ask the waiter to recommend something, he brings you whatever the kitchen has too much of. Not here."

They had pâté to start, then rich bowls of bouillabaisse, then a fish course, then the entree—guinea hen under glass, the dish that had always symbolized the absolute maximum of luxury to Saundra. It was as good as it was luxurious.

Wine with the meal, an elaborate dessert afterward, coffee and brandy. Every dish perfectly prepared, deliciously different, and tastefully served.

"This is a wonderful place," she told Johnny. "I hope I'm not making a pig of myself. I'm not used to dining at Marmaduke's. The Automat is generally more like it for me."

"Finished?" He smiled.

She nodded. "I hope I didn't eat too much. I hope I can get up from the table."

He laughed, and she got up easily from the table. Johnny signed for the check, left a twenty dollar tip, and they left the restaurant. She thought about the tip—twenty dollars was one hell of a lot to leave a waiter.

But, if the bill was one hundred dollars plus tax, twenty dollars was less than twenty percent.

It was something to think about.

"Ready for the main course, Saundra?"

"You mean the . . . nightclub?"

"That's right."

"I'm ready," she said.

The tuxedoed doorman at Marmaduke's did not trouble himself to hail cabs for customers. Johnny caught the cab himself and they piled into it. Johnny gave the address and Saundra noticed something rather startling.

The cabbie was Rick Noscaasi, the man whom she had so elaborately seduced in Central Park just Thursday night. She hoped he wouldn't recognize her.

But, when they arrived at the given address and the cabbie turned to collect his fare, he *did* recognize her. A shadow of remembrance crossed his face and he smiled briefly and secretly. But he said nothing.

Then they were out of the cab. "This way," Johnny was saying, leading her to another brownstone not much different from the one that had housed Marmaduke's. There was, however, one significant difference. This building had no windows. Sandstone could easily guess the reason for this.

Johnny took a key from his pocket and opened a heavy oak door. He let her inside, followed her and closed the door. "The key is the membership card," he explained. "Like a bottle club. Except there's a difference."

They walked together up a long flight of stairs.

"IT MUST BE very interesting," Joe Jeffers said. "Working for a publishing house, I mean. But then again I may be projecting. When I was fresh out of college I wanted to write for a living. I tried a little. I was lousy. So it seemed to me that the next best thing to writing would be working with writers."

"It's challenging," Marilyn admitted.

"What sort of stuff do you publish?"

"Trash."

He looked up, surprised.

"Rubbish," she repeated. "Slushy magazines for suburban housewives. Cheesecake magazines for old men and pimply adolescents to drool over. True detective magazines to satisfy sadists and inspire criminals. Phulcorte isn't exactly the Tiffany's of Publisher's Row. Gems we do not publish. Garbage is our stock in trade."

"And you enjoy it?"

"I don't enjoy the junk that comes into the office," she said. "It's more a case of enjoying the job itself. Working my way up, doing a good job, that sort of thing."

"Think you're getting places?"

"I think so. I'm moving up pretty rapidly. Publishing used to be a rotten racket for a woman. Man's world and all that. Now it's different, mainly because a good man can make more dough in advertising or public relations. And—hey, what is this? I'm beginning to feel as though this is a job interview instead of a date!"

He laughed. "You're right," he said. "I didn't mean to be a pest. And you've hardly touched your steak. I've kept you too busy peppering you with questions. We'll both shut up and eat now, okay?"

She picked up knife and fork and went at it.

She was beginning to understand why it was so damnably easy for her to feel relaxed with Joe around. He was not the sort of man who got disturbed easily. He was calm, easy-going. He did what he wanted to do without a worry in the world. Eating every meal at the steakhouse was a part of it. Other men would feel compelled to try a different restaurant every night if they lived in a city like New York, or if they were visiting there. But Joe had found the place he preferred, and he ate there consistently. He was happy that way.

He was not a man who put up a false front. He didn't wear his heart on his sleeve, didn't walk around with his insides hanging out. But whatever part of himself he revealed was revealed honestly. As a result, Marilyn didn't feel compelled to pretend. She was herself—for better or for worse—and it was nice that way.

"Do you have any children?" she asked over coffee. The coffee very black and very full-bodied, better than what she made at home.

"None. We wanted to, but—"

He let the sentence trail off and she waited for him to pick it up again.

"Janice couldn't. It wasn't a permanent condition, according to the doctor. She would have been able to have children in time. But she didn't get the time."

"I shouldn't have brought it up."

"I don't mind talking about it."

"But—"

"I'm serious. A person can react to tragedy or loneliness in one of two ways. He can turn himself inside-out and hide from the world and quit trying. Or he can rear back and fight. I had one store when Janice died. Now I have five. It was the only outlet I had and I poured myself into it. I worked like a truck horse. Harder than most truck horses at that, come to think of it. I couldn't build a home and I couldn't build a family so I built a business. It was better than withdrawing, better than trying to close my eyes. Now the pain is gone. There's still a scar, I suppose. They tell you the scars never vanish completely. But the pain stopped."

She pictured him, swallowing his grief and working his way through it. He was the sort of man she could admire. Most men were weak on the inside, weaker than most women. Most men in the twentieth century were appallingly short on guts. Joe Jeffers was a different sort of man.

"You fit the same mold," he said suddenly. "You're a very lonely woman, aren't you?"

"What makes you say that?"

He shrugged easily. "You work too hard to be happy," he told her. "You push too strenuously. Look at the way you're throwing yourself into that job of yours. And it's not even a job you like—"

"I like my job."

"Do you?"

She stared.

"I get a different impression," he said. "I don't think you like your job at all. I think you're using it to escape from yourself. I think—"

Her eyes were very wide when suddenly he broke off and shrugged again. "I'm sorry," he said. "Sometimes I talk too much."

"I don't think so."

"Let's drop it," he said. "Where would you like to go now? I couldn't get tickets to anything, didn't have the time. But we ought to be able to pick up a pair to something from one of the specs. Or would you rather go to a nightclub? Jazz, dancing—you name it."

"Well—"

"Anything you want."

She lit a cigarette. "We can do anything I want?"

"Anything. Well, anything within some semblance of reason. We can't take a trip to the moon, much as I'd like to. We can't go prospecting for gold in the Klondike. Outside of those two limitations we can do anything you want."

"You sure?"

"Positive."

"Well," Marilyn said, "I thought maybe we could spend a quiet evening at home."

"What?"

"Go back to my apartment," she said. "We've got a good hi-fi and a stack of records ranging from Bach to Bartok and from Bunk to Monk. Plus Gregorian chants, Hindu water music, a bagpipe ensemble and a sports car race. The chants and the water music are Joan's because she is far-out and the bagpipes and sports cars are Saundra's because she is nuts."

She drew on the cigarette. "I don't feel like painting the town," she went on. "Or seeing a show or running around or anything else. I enjoy talking to you. I'd like to take you home and talk some more."

"I'd like that."

"Would you?"

"Uh-huh." He smiled gently. "I'll probably get disturbing ideas," he said. "I'll probably get desirous. I might even make a pass at you, Marilyn."

"I might encourage you."

"Really?"

"Uh-huh."

"Sounds like fun."

"It will be fun," she said. "Let's go, Joe."

They went.

WHILE SAUNDRA STONE dined with Johnny Lipton at Marmaduke's, and while Marilyn Harper dined with Joe Jeffers at Keen's, Joan McKay sat in Riker's munching a cheeseburger. She kept the cheeseburger company with soggy French fries and a cup of battery acid that the management laughingly called coffee.

This particular Riker's was just two blocks from the apartment, and it was a good thing. This alone recommended the place. Joan finished the cheeseburger, partially finished the French fries, and attempted the coffee.

Then she left.

The picture still danced in her head, but now the picture had taken a turn for the worse. Before her sojourn at Riker's she had stopped back at the apartment. Marilyn was there, and Joe Jeffers came by to pick Marilyn up, and before Joe arrived Joan saw Marilyn's bare body, and then the two of them left, and now here she was. The effect was distressing.

There was only one cure and she intended to take the cure as quickly as possible. She hurried back to the apartment, cooled off under the shower, and dressed. Joan was not much of a clothes-horse—the job certainly didn't demand it—but she did possess a Best Dress, and this was what she wore. The dress was blood red and it made her look slightly magnificent, accentuating breasts and hips, showing her legs (which were good legs) and contrasting nicely with her blonde hair.

She wore stockings and her highest heels. She dabbed expensive perfume under each breast and into each armpit and behind each ear.

The sexual aspect.

She shook her hair loose from its severe bun and let it spill down over her shoulders. She brushed it and brushed it and brushed it until it glistened. She topped it off with a saucy red hat that matched the dress. When she surveyed the results of all this careful preparation in the mirror she was pleased. She looked lovely, damn it.

You're pretty, she told herself. You're very pretty, and tonight you are going to go out on the town and find yourself a girl. A girl as pretty as yourself, with a little bit of luck. A real bomb of a girl with boobs out to here and a pinchable behind.

And you are going to score.

She sighed. She was sounding like a sailor on his first liberty since World War II. But she couldn't help the way she felt. She was hungry, hungry for a woman.

Starving.

She left the apartment, elevated back down to earth again, and walked to Park Avenue where she was able to catch a cab. The look the cabdriver gave her testified to the effect of her preparations. He looked as though he'd love to take her to a hotel instead.

She told him to cruise down Second Avenue. He did this, and at the corner of 52nd Street she found the place she was looking for. It was a cocktail lounge, blatantly sophisticated on the outside, cutely named The Green Door after a classic piece of twentieth century American vulgarity.

"Right here," she said.

The Green Door was infinitely more subtle than The Open d'Or, the Village dive where she had picked up Terri. The sloppy trappings of pseudo-bohemianism of The Open d'Or gave way to smartness and suavity. A jet black carpet covered the floor from wall to wall. The ceiling was also black, and the walls were white. The result of this rather outré paint job was that the room seemed much wider and the ceiling much shorter than was actually the case.

The tables were all black except for the very top surface, which was white. The chairs were totally black. There were perhaps a dozen tables. There was also a black bar with six or seven stools around it. Music came over a P.A. system rather than through a jukebox. There was a small spinet piano on a raised stage but no one was playing it.

It was a place that catered to lesbians, but it was not a rathole by any stretch of the imagination. Here were congregated the lesbians who lived on the fashionable East Side, lesbians with money, lesbians with top jobs in fashion or design or industry. The Green Door was not just a place to pick up a girl. It was a place to have a drink, a place to relax.

A slender usherette in a charcoal gray suit led Joan to an empty table. Her buttocks swayed prettily as she walked. Joan repressed an urge to reach out and pinch the girl's bottom. There would be time later for that sort of thing. Before the evening was over she would have a girl to caress, a girl with a bottom to pinch and breasts to kiss and—

She ordered a stinger and sipped it when it arrived. It was good. It got the Riker's taste out of her mouth.

A male homosexual with an absurd mince appeared from out of the woodwork and seated himself at the piano. He began to play Rodgers and Hart tunes, starting with "Mountain Greenery" and moving on from there. By the time he had switched to Cole Porter, the ball was rolling. A girl detached herself from the mob at the bar and came over to Joan's table.

The girl was magnificent. That was the first impression Joan received, before she noticed what, exactly, the girl looked like, what she was wearing, the color of her hair and eyes, the shape of her body. She was simply magnificent.

Then she noticed the rest. The girl was a tall brunette with eyes that were almost black. The girl had a fashion model's figure—small in the breasts and hips but very elaborately constructed, very neatly put together. Sleek lines, an altogether pleasing appearance A tiny rosebud mouth with just a hint of lipstick. A face of pale beauty.

"Pardon me," the vision was saying. "May I join you?"

"Of course."

The vision sat down. "I saw you here," she began, timidly. You looked lonely. I thought perhaps you *were* alone, in which case you might welcome some companionship."

"I was lonely," Joan admitted. "And it's nice to sit with someone. Very nice."

It was hard to talk. Very hard. Try talking with your heart in your mouth. It's not easy.

"My name's Lucia," the vision said. "Lucia Thomas."

"Joan."

"Joan?"

"Joan Breckenridge," Joan McKay said.

"Do you come here often, Joan?"

"Not very often."

"I don't think I've ever seen you before."

"I've never seen you," Joan said. "If I had, I would remember it. I wouldn't forget."

"You're sweet, Joan."

The pianist switched to "You're the Tops" and Lucia Thomas sang along with him:

"You're the end,

"You're the boobs on Venus;

"You're the most,

"You're Apollo's—"

"Happy days," Lucia said. "Happy, happy days. This place is frighteningly symbolic, wouldn't you say? A contradiction, really. Everything is either white or black. That's all—nothing but black and white. And the world isn't like that. There are all shades of gray. Who should know about those shades of gray better than we? The grayness is our lives."

For an insane moment Joan thought this girl was reading poetry from *Agony*. The funny part of it was that Lucia Thomas could get away with dialogue like this while other girls would fall on their separate faces.

"They call this place The Green Door. But the door isn't green at all. Did you notice that?"

"I hadn't noticed."

"That's what's so amusing," Lucia said. "The door is red. Red is the complement of green, of course. The opposite number on the color wheel. And do you know what you get if you mix red and green together?"

"What?"

"Gray. Isn't that interesting?"

Joan nodded and finished her drink. She couldn't even follow the conversation any more. Her head was beginning to swim—not from the drink but from the sheer dynamism of Lucia Thomas.

She ached to touch the girl, longed to run her own hands over that slim and milk-white figure. Her lips hungered to kiss the girl's breasts. The picture was reshaped once again in her mind. She was still the blonde, but now the brunette was Lucia. And the man, of course, had been neatly snipped away.

"Do you live in Manhattan, Joan?"

"Yes."

"East Side?"

She shook her head. "Downtown," she said. "On Bank Street in the Village."

"You like it there?"

"Very much."

Lucia smiled easily. She must have been close to thirty, Joan decided. And she was the sort of woman who somehow grew increasingly desirable as she grew older.

"I lived downtown once," Lucia said. "Long ago. Years. I understand it's changed in the past five years. Or maybe I've changed. It's hard to say."

Joan said nothing.

"Do you work, Joan?"

"I write poetry." It was a convenient lie, even partially true. She made it a point to leave *Agony* out of her extracurricular activities. True, her job might impress some people. But she was more interested in keeping the two worlds apart. Hence the lies.

"Have you been published?"

"No."

"You will be. I understand that all it takes is time and application. And talent, of course. Keep working and keep submitting and you'll crack into print."

"Do you write?"

"God, no." Lucia laughed. "I'm an overpaid, underfed, overdressed clothes horse. I dress in over-priced garbage and hip-swiveling faggots take pictures of me and run them in fashion books. It's a panic, darling. All those nice suburban housewives looking at pictures of a gay girl cast in the role of the eternal female. No, I'm not a writer. But I've known writers. Possibly some you've heard of."

There was a sudden flash of illumination.

"Look," Joan said suddenly. "Look, you don't have to be nice to me or impress me or anything. Really, you don't. I'm flattered, but it's not necessary. I think you're the most beautiful thing I've ever set eyes on and I'd like nothing better than to go to bed with you. So just relax."

"Well," Lucia said. "Well. You're honest, dear. I'm not used to honesty. You're so lovely and so sweet and so much a woman that I—"

Joan took Lucia's hand.

"Let's get out of here," she said, breathlessly. "Let's go to your apartment. Let's take off all of our clothes and get into bed. Then let's make love. Mad love, wild love, sweet love that lasts all night."

Joan insisted on paying for her own drink. They left the club—and Joan noticed on the way out that the door really *was* red—and they got into a cab.

"Ten Park Avenue," Lucia said.

On the way to Lucia's apartment they necked like high school kids.

Chapter Six

CALL IT NOTHING, for this club had no name.

There was no club charter, and there were no club offi-cers, and there was no official membership list. There was a post office box where the annual dues were sent. Someone emptied this box, but he was nameless and faceless. There were membership cards in the form of keys like the one with which Johnny Lipton had opened the heavy oak door. These keys were special and hard to duplicate, but for insurance a small stoop-shouldered man stood in the darkness on the landing to check each visitor and make sure he was a member. The man's appearance was damned deceptive. He looked weak, spineless, and inches away from death by starvation. Once a healthy and slightly drunken ox, a former right guard on the Cleveland Browns, had tried to crash a meeting. The small stoop-shoul-dered man had asked him to leave, and the ox had laughed, whereupon the little man had thrown the ox down the flight of stairs with resultant multiple fractures of the collarbone, both legs, and one arm. The little man did not carry a gun or a knife or a sap. He did not need one.

He smiled gently at Johnny and Saundra and they walked

past him. They climbed another flight of stairs, then walked quickly over a thickly-carpeted floor to an entrance way. Johnny led the redhead into a small curtained booth. The same wine-red carpet covered the floor of the booth. Two plush leather chairs faced the curtain. A divan, low and long, reposed sensuously along one wall.

Johnny pointed to a chair. Saundra sat down and he sat down in the other chair beside her. Her brain was buzzing and she felt a little bit lost. Unless she was mistaken, this seemed like anything in the world but a sex show. She'd had visions of a table at a swank and subtle nightclub with plenty to drink and an awe-inspiring floor show.

But what was happening? It looked for all the world like a rather round-about experiment in seduction. A quiet booth, probably soundproof. A couch to make it upon. Chairs to sit in beforehand.

Johnny drew the curtain.

At that point she got the message. The curtained wall of the booth was not a wall at all. It was open, and the booth was miraculously transformed into a box seat like the boxes at the opera. Johnny's box was an especially good one. It was right at the side of the small stage, very close to the scene of the action which, he assured her in a whisper, would begin at any moment.

"Take off your clothes," he said. "Don't worry—no one from the stage can see into any of the boxes. It's more exciting to watch it in the nude."

They stripped. Sandstone felt very strange. There was something unreal about the entire episode thus far and she could not pin it down, could not say for certain what was bothering her. For the first time she was beginning to feel insecure in her attempt at ensnaring Johnny Lipton in the noble bonds of matrimony.

Not that she doubted her own charms. Not that she doubted Johnny Lipton's interest in her charms, or his determination to take advantage of those charms. But the man seemed so damned sure of himself, so confident, that it was going to be tough to make him want her on a permanent basis.

And right now he was ignoring her completely. Any other man in a similar situation would be all over her by now, hands on her body, mouth on her mouth. Not Johnny Lipton. He wasn't even looking at her, as a matter of fact. He was ignoring her so thoroughly that she felt inadequate. His eyes were focused upon the empty stage.

A spotlight illuminated a circle in the center of the stage.

A girl materialized from out of nowhere, stood in the center of the blue spot, smiled into the darkness that was the audience. There was a rustle of applause and the girl bowed ever so slightly. She was a tall blonde, leggy and hippy and busty, with a very red mouth. She wore a simple black cocktail dress.

"The mistress of ceremonies," Johnny explained in a whisper. "Her name is Andrea."

"Welcome," the blonde was saying. "Welcome one and welcome all. You're just in time for our show. We've got some brand-new performers and we're sure you'll like the show. If you're alone and at any time in the proceedings desire companionship, just press the buzzer. That's all for now."

Andrea vanished.

There was movement in the shadows on the side of the stage. Then a girl came into view, a short girl with long jet-black hair. She moved into the spotlight and Sandstone saw that she was very dark, probably Puerto Rican. She was dressed as a juvenile delinquent type, with skin-tight blue jeans, tennis shoes, and a tight yellow sweater.

The Puerto Rican girl put both hands on her hips and began to do a sort of bump-and-grind at the audience. The standard movement of the burlesque stripper was incongruous now when performed by a girl in blue jeans and a sweater. Somehow a motion which had become conventional was rendered vulgar by the girl's attire. She winked broadly at the audience, then suddenly cupped her breasts in her hands and began to squeeze them.

Saundra stared at her. The girl kept toying with her own breasts. They were very large breasts, and her handling of them seemed to be having an effect. She moved her hands and Saundra saw nipples outlined in sharp relief, plainly visible through the yellow sweater. The girl threw her shoulders back and stretched.

The girl began to speak to the audience, in a slow drawl.

"I wan' a man," she announced. "I wan' a man to come an' love me. You know how I mean? Tha's want I wan.'"

The girl's hands, poised once again on her breasts began to travel very slowly downward over her flat stomach.

Then the man appeared.

He was a Negro, very dark, well over six feet tall, broad-shouldered and muscled. The teenage-gang notion was preserved now. The Negro's dress also suited the skit—he wore heavy stomping boots on his feet, tight blue jeans, a white tee-shirt and a black leather jacket. He smiled.

And moved toward the girl. He moved very slowly, deliberately.

The Negro boy and the Puerto Rican girl began to get into the spirit of things. He took her in his arms and kissed her. His huge hands found her breasts and played with them. She gasped.

Saundra gasped with her.

Each of the two performers undressed the other. The Negro drew the girl's sweater up over her head. He tugged her blue jeans down over her hips and ripped her panties to shreds. Then he stood up and let her strip him, interrupting her periodically.

Saundra wondered whether they were just acting, just playing out parts, or whether they enjoyed the roles they played. They certainly seemed to enjoy what they were doing. As far as she could see, both the man and the girl were enjoying themselves immensely. They seemed genuinely excited.

They were young, she realized. Very young. The girl, de-spite her physical maturity, could not have been more than seventeen, eighteen at the very most. The boy was about the same age, perhaps a year older.

Now they were both naked.

The girl lay down on the floor, the man beside her, kissing her and caressing her.

The girl went into a complex backbend. Slowly and sensuously she elevated her body until her entire weight was supported solely by her hands and her feet.

Now the boy began caressing her body in earnest.

"IT'S AWKWARD, ISN'T it?" Marilyn smiled. "It seemed like a good idea, didn't it? Come up to my apartment, sit around, relax. So here we are. Music on the hi-fi, drinks at our elbows, and it's nerve-wracking. I'm sorry."

"Don't be silly."

"I'm being serious. We're both sitting around waiting for somebody to make a pass so that we can jump into bed together. It's breaking wrong, I suppose."

"I'm enjoying myself," Joe Jeffers said.

"Are you?"

"Yes."

"What's to enjoy?"

"Being with you. That's all."

She joined him on the couch. He slipped an arm around her and she leaned back to relax against it.

"I have to go back to Kansas City," he told her. "Too soon. I don't want to go back."

"Enchanted by the big city?"

"Uh-uh."

"What, then?"

"Enchanted by you."

She laughed. "It's a temporary sort of enchantment," she said. "As soon as you get on the plane I turn into a pumpkin. Nothing to worry about."

"I think you might like Kansas City," he told her. His voice soft, almost dreamy. This is a bad word for a man's voice, especially a ruggedly masculine man like Joe Jeffers. But his voice had a dreamy quality to it. "It's not a bad town. Doesn't fit the stereotype of the Midwest by any stretch of the imagination. One of the fastest moving towns in the country. The industry is all the sort that calls for skilled labor, you see. The mean salary is very high. No slums, no problems. Big-city opportunities and small-town advantages. A good place to live."

He was getting to dangerous ground.

"You sound like the Chamber of Commerce," she said. "Save the advertisements. I like New York."

"Do you?"

She stared at him.

"You love New York," he said to her. "And you love your job, and you love your single status, and you're the happiest female in the world."

"More or less."

"And I don't believe a word of it."

"Joe—"

"I don't," he said. "You hate your job and you hate New York and you can't stand the life you're living. That's why you push so damned hard. That's why the goal is everything, why you throw yourself head-and-shoulders into every damned thing you do. Why you never hold anything back. Why you had to pick a man up the other night, which man turned out to be me."

"Are you complaining?"

"Not at all. Just making a point. If you liked your job so damned much you'd take it easy. You wouldn't work so hard. That's a fact—did you know it? People who like their jobs take it easy. The hard workers *hate* their jobs. They want to move to some other job, so they work their way out of the job they hate. That's you all over."

She was annoyed. "And your damned stores? The ones you worked like hell building up after your wife died? I suppose you hated them. That's why they've done so well."

"More or less."

"What?"

"The same thing. I didn't like what I was. A little man. I was sick of being a little man. It was all right to be a little man while Janice was alive. Money didn't matter then. Without her, it was all there was. Now I don't hate the stores anymore."

"Now you're a big man?"

"As big as I'll ever be. I make a living. I save money. I make out."

"Congratulations."

He frowned at the bitterness in her voice. "I'm sorry," he said. "Sometimes I have a knack for doing things backwards. I've got you mad at me now. I didn't mean to do that."

"It's all right. I—"

"It's not all right. I didn't mean to pick at you like that. That's not what I was trying to do."

"Well—"

"I was trying something else entirely," Joe said.

"What?"

"Trying to get you to come back to Kay Cee with me."

She stared. "You must be out of your mind."

"Maybe."

"I—"

"It's very simple, really. I don't know why I've been having so much trouble saying it. I met you and you're what I need. Everything I need. It's fast, it's sudden, it probably sounds childish—I can't help it. I am what I am. I think I know you pretty well. It takes some people a lifetime to find out what another person is like. I know what you're like already. I think I knew from the minute I met you. It happened very quickly."

"And now—"

"Now I want you to marry me."

"That's impossible."

"I don't think so."

"Look—"

"I love you, Marilyn."

"That's crazy. You just met me, you don't know me, you don't love me. It's crazy."

"I love you."

She said nothing. Neither did he, and the room was very still. She shook a cigarette loose from her pack and started to light it from the butt of the first. Something made her change her mind. She returned the cigarette unlit to the pack and ground out the butt in the ashtray.

"Marilyn—"

She took a deep breath.

"It would be a good life, honey. You'd like the town. You'd like being my wife."

"I don't want to talk about it."

"I just want you to think about it. I don't expect you to hop on the plane with me. But think about it, let it rattle around in your head a little. You'll see."

"I don't even want to think about it, Joe."

"Why not?"

"Because it's out of the question."

"That's not why. It's because you're afraid. Afraid you might get to like the idea. Afraid you might find out about a brand-new world."

"I don't want to think about it, Joe. Can't you understand me? I don't want to think about it. I want to go to bed."

He grinned mirthlessly. "That's a pretty easy out, isn't it? Roll in the hay so you don't have to think."

"Maybe I'm a whore."

"Marilyn—"

"An emotional whore," she said. "Maybe that's the whole

thing. I don't know. I don't want to know. All I know is that I want to go to bed with you. Now."

He stood up and she went to him, buried her face in his chest, let his arms hold her and soothe her. *Roll in the hay so you don't have to think.* But that wasn't it, not now, not when he was holding her. She wanted him, wanted him desperately, and it wasn't an escape, wasn't a dodge, wasn't anything more or less than passion, more or less than blind animal hunger.

His chest crushed her breasts and it was delicious.

"Joe—"

Now he was kissing her. His mouth tasted good, sweet, and she hugged him close while her tongue tasted the goodness and sweetness of his mouth. Then she released him, slipped away from him, and took him by the hand.

They walked to the bedroom.

"Be good for me," she whispered. "I need you so much, Joe. Let's not think about anything, let's stop thinking altogether, let's just make love. Make love to me, Joe."

ON THE STAGE, the Negro boy and the Puerto Rican girl performed with an enviable combination of skill and agility and zeal. The rather lovely position of their first encounter, with the girl supporting herself via a magnificent backbend and the boy riding bareback, as it were, was not the sum total of their repertoire.

They had a bagful of tricks.

They also had, evidently, an inexhaustible supply of energy. They made love twice more, in two new and ingenious methods, and then the first part of the proceedings was more or less over. Saundra was startled when the two of them stood up, bowed briefly, and were received with a deluge of applause—hand clapping, whistles and cheers—from all parts of the "theater."

The applause was a definite shock to Saundra. Throughout the performance she had had the distinct feeling that she and Johnny were the only observers, that the performers were unaware of their presence. She knew it was a ridiculous notion but it was inevitable. There was something intensely private about the whole thing. She felt like a peeping Tom.

The applause stopped at once. The Negro boy and the Puerto Rican girl settled down for Act Two, which was about to start. And start it did, with a very small blonde girl joining the pair in center stage.

Now Saundra knew damned well that some people look much younger than they actually are. She also knew that makeup can take years off a person's age.

But this, she knew just as well, did not alter by one iota the fact that the little blonde was not and could not be a day over fourteen years old.

What was a fourteen-year-old doing in a sex show?

The answer to that question came quite quickly. The answer came quite dynamically, for that matter, because the Negro boy and the Puerto Rican girl came to life at once, jumping toward the little blonde.

And the blonde cowered in brilliantly simulated fear. She turned to run but she could not move quickly enough. The boy caught her around the waist and spun her around neatly. The dark girl slapped her in the face. The slap rang throughout the theater.

"Strip her," the boy said. "Let's see what she looks like. Rip her clothes."

The Puerto Rican girl ripped the blonde's clothing off. She tore the white blouse open, exposing small plump breasts. She took a breast in each hand and squeezed.

The blonde moaned.

"Mine are bigger," the Puerto Rican girl said. "You wan' to see the differen'?"

The Puerto Rican girl stooped down to rub her own big breasts against the blonde's little breasts. Then she straightened up, laughed happily, and bent once more to remove the girl's blue jeans. The blonde was not wearing any panties.

Now the boy changed his grip, his arm moving so that he held the blonde by her breasts. Meanwhile the Puerto Rican girl stooped down and began to amuse herself with the blonde.

The blonde screamed.

It was a shrill scream, not too loud and not too soft, perfectly calculated indeed so that it was as loud as it could be without being audible outside of that particular building. The blonde had spent considerable time practicing so that she could scream at just the right pitch.

Saundra, of course, did not realize this.

The girl's shrill scream went through her like a knife.

Saundra watched, fascinated. This was a new one on her. Saundra could not be called a girl who was lacking in a rudimentary understanding of the highways and byways of sex. In some circles she was reckoned an expert. But lesbian activity lay outside her ken. She watched now, struck dumb, as the Puerto Rican girl did unmentionable things to the blonde while the Negro boy gripped the blonde relentlessly.

At last it was over.

"My turn now," the Negro boy said. "My turn, baby. You hold her down while I get my kicks."

The two of them forced the blonde to the floor. The Puerto Rican girl sat on the blonde's face while the Negro boy made love to the blonde. Saundra watched the whole performance. It was really getting to her now. She wanted to be in Johnny's arms, experiencing the delights of his embrace.

And at the same time she wanted to go on watching.

Saundra stared. Her heart raced.

She glanced across at Johnny Lipton. He was sitting beside her, sitting in the other chair that was exactly like hers, sitting as nude as Saundra herself.

He was smiling.

LUCIA HAD A nice apartment.

How's that for understatement? Take the ultimate in luxury and combine with it the ultimate in chic, and place the result on the top floor of a Park Avenue apartment building, and what you wind up with is Lucia's apartment.

They were in the bedroom.

Now it is a very easy matter to consider passion. It is easy to enumerate strokes and pokes, to catalogue moans and groans. It is not hard at all to speak knowingly of kisses and sighs.

But this was something else.

This was the afterglow, the warmth and pleasure after it was all over. And this was a different prospect entirely. They were not making love.

Now they were finished.

Together.

And glowing.

Joan McKay—Joan Breckenridge, for this evening at least—lay with her head on the outflung arm of Lucia Thomas. Joan's eyes were closed. Her breathing had just recently returned to normal; her pulse rate was still a little higher than it generally was. There was the ghost of an involuntary smile upon her lips.

Her arms felt like leaden weights. Her legs were entirely numb.

She felt divine.

I needed this, she thought. God, how I needed it! Freud was right, the sex urge is the biggest thing going, it's too big to fight.

She stretched very slowly, gingerly, like a cat upon awakening. Her arms and legs tingled pleasantly now. She rolled over slightly and looked at Lucia.

Lucia was beautiful.

Lucia was also awake. Her head was on a foam-rubber pillow. She was smoking a cigarette in a holder. The holder was black and looked like ebony.

"I sometimes think," Lucia said, "that the cardinal purpose of sexual congress is one of making tobacco truly enjoyable. A cigarette tastes much better after love. Have you ever noticed that?"

Joan had never noticed that. She had never thought much about it, if the truth be known, but she was willing to learn. She accepted a cigarette from Lucia.

It tasted fine.

"I feel so lazy," Lucia said. "So very lazy. I couldn't move if my life depended upon it, I don't think. That was good, baby, so good."

Joan didn't say anything.

"Was it good for you, too?"

"Wonderful."

"I know it was," Lucia said. "I could tell. It wouldn't have been that good for me if it hadn't been good for you. It was perfect for us, baby."

"Perfect."

"And how do you feel now?"

"Wonderful."

"Well—"

Now Lucia was kissing her. A gentle, searching kiss, mouths closed, bodies warmly touching.

I don't even like this girl, she thought. She's not too

bright—suave, but not bright. And she's not very nice and she's a bore. But she's exciting. God, is she exciting!

Then hands gripped her breasts.

Then a mouth began to excite her.

And then they were making love.

It was different this time, not as hectic, not as furious. But it was just as moving, every bit as moving, maybe even better because there was something very fine about the calmness that took the place of earlier hunger.

It was good.

The afterglow was also different. The feeling of having fallen from Mount Everest into a pile of goose feathers was modified this time, changed to a briefer fall. Warmth rather than exhaustion was the main thing involved in the afterglow.

"Joan Breckenridge," Lucia whispered. "You're fine, Joan Breckenridge. You're very fine. I want you to stay all night, my baby. Close to me."

Could she? The worst result would be that the girls would suspect she'd found herself a man. Nothing, then, to worry about. And it would be pleasant to stay the night.

"I'll stay."

"I knew you would. I like having you around, Joan Breckenridge."

"I like being with you."

"I love you, Joan. I'm not just saying it."

Silence.

"I love you, Joan Breckenridge."

"I love you, Lucia."

But my name's not Breckenridge, Joan McKay thought. *And I don't love you at all.*

Chapter Seven

THE LIGHTS WENT out on the stage. The blue spotlight shone no more. The little blonde, the Puerto Rican girl, the Negro boy—all vanished. They took no curtain calls, stole no bows. They simply packed up and left.

And Johnny Lipton drew the curtain in the small booth. He flicked a switch on the wall and a soft red glow illuminated the booth. He turned to Saundra and smiled.

She was naked and he was naked and they sat side by side in identical red leather chairs. There was something inane about it all, and Saundra knew that without the stimulation of the performance they just watched, the present situation would be a laughable state of affairs. But the show had done its work. She could not laugh now. She was too keyed up.

It was ridiculous, all right. Ludicrous, certainly. Absurd, to be sure. They were calmly nude, and now they were supposed to fall breathless together to the divan, there to consummate their panting desire and quench their monumental thirst. On paper it added up to the most bizarre stupidity since Lot's daughter knocked one off with the old man, but in practice it was different. On paper it was dry and sterile, but they were not on paper.

They were on the divan.

On the divan. They got there simply enough. Johnny smiled a second time, and Johnny murmured: "Let's lie down on the divan."

Incredible.

There was the inevitable moment of awkward stupidity, during which they both perhaps wondered what they were doing together on the divan. But Johnny saved things. His hands roamed Saundra's body, and that did it.

Saundra moaned gently. Her arms went around him, drawing him close, pressing his chest to hers. The sensation sent little quivers of delight jolting through her.

Good.

Very good.

Excellent.

She rolled over onto her side and he lay on his side, facing her. His hands reached around her, holding her shoulders, then brushing down over her back. He gripped her and squeezed gently. It was extremely exciting.

"You have a marvelous backside," he whispered. "A truly spectacular one. In case no one has told you."

She pouted. "Don't you like my breasts?"

"Of course I do. You have spectacular breasts as well. I'm just complimenting your backside. Breasts aren't everything, you know. It's the Oedipus instinct in the contemporary male, that's all."

He was strange, she thought. He liked to talk while he prepared to make love. Perhaps that was one important prereq-uisite if she wanted to marry him. Perhaps she ought to make cheerful conversation in the sack, and this would make a warm spot for her in his heart. It was a thought.

But it was damned difficult to make bubbling conversa-tion when he was setting her aflame with those clever little hands of his.

"Aren't there other areas?"

"Hmmmm?"

"Other areas," she said. "Other unappreciated areas de-serving of masculine attention."

Now she was talking like him.

"There are," he said.

"Well—"

"Like this," he said.

It would not be easy to make any more clever conversation.

"Johnny—"

Very deliberately he rolled her onto her back. His mouth came down upon hers and his tongue reached into her mouth. It was, she realized suddenly, the first and only time he had kissed her.

She wound her arms about him and returned the kiss. Then the kiss ended, and he began.

It was heaven.

Saundra Stone now knew why women like Cleopatra and Madame de Pompadour had been able to exert such an influ-ence upon the history of the world. They were artists of the bedchamber, and such an animal is rare indeed.

Such an animal was now with Saundra Stone.

Because Johnny Lipton was an artist. It may well have been the only thing in the world at which he was the least bit proficient, but it was enough.

He was magnificent.

No one else in the world had even done what he was doing to her. No one else had ever played upon her like Heifetz upon a Stradivarius, working wonders, making miracles, doing things that had never been done before.

Slowly.

Then faster.

Then slowly again.

He brought her, racing and trembling, to the very peak of pleasure. But just at the precipice he would halt, slow down, denying her the release she craved so desperately. He would slow down, and she would be tense with need, and then he would begin to raise her once more until her senses were turning inside out and she had reached an even higher peak than before.

Then he would let her down again.

It was the most phenomenal experience of her life. Time and time again she was almost there, inches away from miraculous fulfillment.

And time and time again he left her hanging in the middle of the air.

Until he was ready.

Then he began to excite her once more, until she knew

that it had to happen for her this time or she would simply die on the spot, die of aching and need and pain and frustration. It had to happen, that was all there was to it, it had to happen now or never, had to happen or she would never live through the night.

And then, miraculously, he was letting it happen for her now, was indeed making it happen, and nothing in the world had ever been like this.

It was like nothing and it was like everything.

It was nothing that had gone before; it was everything she had ever wanted, everything she had ever hoped for, everything she had ever dared or not dared to dream of.

It was magnificent.

Then it was over.

IT WAS OVER.

Joe Jeffers slept. But Marilyn did not sleep, could not sleep. She looked at the darkness of the bedroom and listened to his heavy, measured breathing. She wished she could duplicate his actions and roll over into sound sleep. She knew, however, that this would be impossible. It would be hours before she slept.

She sighed.

It had been good for them. It had always been good for them, and this evening was the best of all. They would always be good together, she realized. They would get better as they went along, always better, each time better than the one before it. She knew this for a fact.

Different people work different ways. Some couples are good it first and get a little less good each time. They go through an affair and each love bout is a little less exciting than the one before it, a little more boring, until sack time becomes the hour of monotony for them.

With others the opposite is true, and that is how it would be for her and Joe. Their lovemaking was a sharing experience. It was the type of lovemaking which was good because they were giving to one another, that worked because they felt something for one another. The more time they spent together the better they knew each other. The greater their mutual knowledge, the more complete their horizontal experience became.

This impressed her.

And now, because he wanted her to marry him and live in Kansas City with him, she could not sleep. Now, because he wanted to turn a very wonderful affair into a permanent deal, sleep was out of the realm of possibility. She wanted to sleep, but wishes were not horses and she was a beggar who would not ride.

She sighed again.

There were two courses of action. There was the easy course and there was the hard course, and neither one seemed to appeal to her. She could do one of two things. She could let what might be desire and what might just as easily be love make up her mind for her. She could forget Phulcorte Press, forget the opportunities available on Publisher's Row, forget indeed her fundamental identity as an individual human being, and she could take Joe Jeffers up on his offer.

She could go with him to Kansas City. She could give up career for home and she could marry the man who lay asleep at her side. This would be the easy thing to do. It would be a life not devoid of rewards by any means. There would be many valuable things in such a life. She would become a woman in the full sense of the word. She would bear Joe Jeffers' children and watch them grow up tall and strong and alive. She would make a house turn into a home. She would be a part of a functioning community. She would love a man who loved her, and she would grow old along with him, and she would never be alone.

But it was not all violins and lilacs. She would become a woman, certainly, but she would cease to be a person. There would be no goal. There would be no drive, no ambition. She would be a smoothly functioning robot, a mindless creature who made love and conceived and bore and raised children, a machine which made the bed and did the dishes. She would play canasta with suburban housewives who, when all was said and done, would be the sort of woman which she would turn into in time. She would join the PTA and the League of Women Voters and some church group. And she would go to church, of course.

Did she want that?

She did not.

So there was another alternative, a little harder perhaps,

but another road. She could say to hell with Joe Jeffers, and she could stay in New York, and she could work harder than ever at Phulcorte until she was too big for Phulcorte. She could put the proper knives into the proper backs, and she could push farther and farther ahead, and she could make the right breaks for herself until she landed in the right slot and brought home thirty or forty thousand a year as head editor at a big house.

Then she could bid a fond adieu to Joan McKay and Saundra Stone, buy a posher-than-posh cooperative apartment somewhere, live high, and feel rich. Then she would be somebody very important, and the world would be her oyster.

But would there be any pearls in that oyster?

Probably not.

No, probably not. There would be the same hectic pick-ups, pick-ups of strangers in expensive bars, pick-ups of acquaintances at cocktail parties. A casual affair here and there, a lover who was safely married so that no real relationship could develop, a quick one with a total stranger. Sex taken as a pill, or as a cathartic, loveless sex, amorous miltown.

Was that what she wanted?

No, that was not what she wanted.

Was there anything else?

Yes, there was something else. A combination of the two, an affair with Joe Jeffers with him in Kansas City and her in New York. Every business trip would find him staying with her. And on her vacation she could go to Kay Cee and stay with him. That way she could have her cake while eating it. She could have Joe and Job, Conquest and Career.

Wouldn't that be good?

No, that would not be good.

Why not?

Simple, she thought. Because it would not work out. Because Joe did not want her on that basis, and because she probably would not want Joe on that basis. Because what was getting better and better for them now would no doubt get worse and worse with the passage of time. Because it was a halfway measure, and that sort of thing never stood up over the long run.

Well, what then?

Good question.

What was the answer?

There didn't seem to be one.

She found a pack of cigarettes on the night table and got one going.

Where are we going?

To hell in a bucket.

What's the matter?

Everything.

Should we get married?

No.

Should we break up?

No, again.

Should we let things stay the way they are?

No, No, No!

Then what?

Good question. Which we would like to answer, kind sir, but there is no answer. No answer at all, no answer anywhere in the world, and isn't that a thorough-going kick in the rear?

It is.

Was he right and did she hate her job? Maybe, but she knew that she could not feel entirely alive without it. She was, in a very real sense, a junkie. She had a work habit, and she had a man habit, and now the two were colliding at top speed. They were banging together, and they were giving her a headache, and it was just too goddamned much for her to take.

She ground out the cigarette. Another butt in another ashtray. I am measuring out my life in butted cigarettes. Not in coffee spoons but in butted cigarettes. What's left when the carton's gone? How deep will they bury me? How will the roses smell when we are all blown to hell?

Questions.

Good questions.

She stretched out beside him and tried to sleep again. It didn't work but she tried anyhow. There was obviously nothing else to do.

IT WAS JUST no night for sleeping. Marilyn Harper was not the only girl who was having trouble keeping her eyes shut. Joan McKay was having the same problems. Her lover, also, was sound asleep. Lucia Thomas lay sprawled on her back with her eyes shut. She was snoring.

There was something quite ludicrous in the whole notion

of a snoring lesbian. A doll-like dyke, head tossed back, small breasts pointing prettily at the ceiling, mouth open, snoring. A laughing matter.

Joan was not laughing. She was not laughing because she was not amused. She had too many other thoughts on her mind.

Like Marilyn Harper, Joan was on the brink of decision. She was faced with a choice and she could not make it. Her choice, however, was not a choice between home and career. It was a different choice entirely, although there were psychological similarities.

She had to decide where the hell she was headed.

One thing she knew. The present state of things was simply intolerable. A double life might be fine for some people, but she just wasn't built to take it. She could not be the Vestal Virgin half the time and the Hot Hermaphrodite the other half—it simply wasn't working out. Besides, one of these days she was going to fall on her face. One of these days someone who knew her as the Loveable Lesbian was going to slip into her Vestal Virgin world and things were going to blow up in her face. Or, in reverse, one day she would get a little bit more frustrated than usual and toss a pass at either Saundra or Marilyn, whoever happened to be around at the time. At which time she would land on her ear and that would be that.

Ugh.

She was going to have to go one way or the other. She could become a lesbian all across the board, with an apartment of her own or with a shackup with another lesbian. She could spend all her evenings at gay bars or gay parties, and all her friends would be lesbians like herself.

This was not devoid of appeal. It would be nice to stop pretending, nice to admit what she was and make the best of it.

But it would also be un-nice, to coin a phrase. To be truthful about it, she was not completely proud of what she was. She was quite firmly convinced that it was definitely less than natural to be a woman who slept with women. While she led her double life, she could at least pretend half the time that she was normal, a woman like Saundra or Marilyn. If she went completely over the bridge, that would be the end of the pretense of normality. She would be a dyke all the way, and she didn't know if she could take it.

It would be unpleasant to be an object of disgust for the world at large.

Could she take it?

She didn't think so.

What then?

Well, every coin had two sides. If she could not renounce the veneer of normality, she could at least renounce lesbianism. She could simply give it up—stop sleeping with girls, stop picking up or being picked up by lesbians.

Just like that.

The trouble was, this would not be the same as breaking any old habit. Giving up sex was not like giving up smoking, which in itself was difficult enough. And if she gave up sex, just dropped the whole thing and found a way to direct her energy into another channel entirely, she would only succeed in turning herself into an old maid before her time. She would be a sexless and useless creature, good for nothing, and that would be no solution. She might as well sew herself up, or go to a doctor for a non-essential hysterectomy.

God!

There was one other answer.

Which frightened her.

It was a simple answer. She could turn from a lesbian into a normal woman. She could sleep with men rather than with girls. She could do what society accepted—turn into a normal, human, heterosexual woman.

Which, she thought disconsolately, was a hell of a lot easier said than done.

Now, lying in bed while Lucia snored disturbingly beside her, she tried to imagine what it would be like with a man. She was fairly certain that, whatever it was like, she would not enjoy it in the least. The idea of a man ripping her, tearing her, using her as a receptacle—this scared her. She could not possibly associate it with pleasure for herself. She thought of the things Saundra and Marilyn did and found it out of the question that what brought them pleasure would bring pleasure to her.

It wouldn't work.

She closed her eyes and tried to concentrate. Her brow furrowed and her breasts heaved with deep breathing. She was a virgin, if not the Vestal Virgin she was supposed to be, and she had never gone all the way with a man or boy. But at the same time she was not totally devoid of experience. She had dated rather actively before a girl at Wessex had taught her what sort of woman she was. Sometimes she had necked or petted.

What had it been like?

She remembered the way boys kissed, and she remembered the way their hands had felt upon her breasts, and she realized with something of a start that what she had done with boys was really not much different than what she had done with girls. Only the final act itself was basically different. There was the fact that men themselves did not excite her. But perhaps this was only a psychological wall she herself had erected. Maybe she was heterosexual, or at least bisexual, and maybe she could make a normal woman of herself if she gave herself the chance.

It was still as frightening as it had ever been. It was still pain and blood and screaming, everything she had always feared so much. But after the first time there would never be any more pain or blood. She might grow to enjoy it. She was built no differently from other girls. She had the same shape, the same organs. She was not like the butches, the mannish lesbians, with flat chests and boyish bodies and coarse hair and masculine features. Only her desires were unnatural.

Perhaps they would change.

And yet she knew that the change would never be a complete one. She might learn to enjoy the embrace of a man, but she was firmly convinced that she could not take the same degree of pleasure from such an embrace that she could receive in the arms of a woman. She might be able to "change over"—she would never know one way or the other until she had tried—but she would never be as satisfied that way.

Never.

She could take the plunge. She could try the big switch, find out what it was like with a man, see if it was good or bad for her. All she had to do was steel herself against pain, steel herself against all the psychological blocks which had been built up within her, steel herself and submit. That was all.

Because, in any event, she could not stay where she was. That much was intolerable. She would have to be a lesbian all the way or be a lesbian not at all. A total lesbian could have some measure of love. A total lesbian could achieve a greater measure of satisfaction than one who hid her peculiarity and gratified her desires only on certain days.

She would find out. She would locate a man, a logical guinea pig for her selfish experiment, and she would use him to determine which role she could play for the rest of her life. If the sexual experience with the man was just barely tolerable, then she would try again. And if it became good, girls like Lucia and Terri and all the others would never see her again.

If not, she would go all the way. Her own apartment. Her own circle of lesbian friends.

One way or the other.

She wondered which it would be.

JOHNNY LIPTON AND Saundra Stone were still on the divan.

As one may have gathered, the three girls who lived at 105 East 73rd Street had a few things in common. Now, like Marilyn Harper and Joan McKay. Sandstone was on the brink of decision. She was trying to make up her mind what to do next.

She was lying with her body next to Johnny's. She was glowing with the aftermath of the most magnificent sexual experience she had ever known in her life, which is saying a lot. And she was making plans.

If she had wanted to marry Johnny Lipton before, this desire was now multiplied a hundred-fold. The idea of spending every night with a man like that was staggering. It might well kill her, but there could not possibly be a better way to die.

But a man like Johnny had obviously been around. A man like Johnny could obviously have all the love he wanted. So if she wanted to make herself indispensable, she had to be better than anything he had ever had before. She had to be so good that he would not be willing to give her up.

She knew just what she was going to do.

She kissed his cheek. He started to stir and she kissed him again.

"Lie still," she told him. "Don't move."

Then she began to kiss him some more. She kissed his closed eyes, his face, his neck. Her lips ran over the skin on his throat.

He smiled with his eyes shut tight.

Her lips moved to his chest. She was going to do something she had never done before, something she guessed very few girls would be willing to do. It was not a thing which particularly appealed to her, but if it accomplished its aim it was well worth it.

She moved lower.

It was part of her plan.

Lower—

HE TOOK HER home in the cab, walked her to her door. They made small talk on the way but she barely listened to what he said to her and had no idea what her answers were. She turned at the door and he drew her close and kissed her.

"I'll see you," he said.

And left.

She was jubilant in the elevator to the apartment. It had been perfect—she had played her cards right and she was going to rake in the pot very shortly. He wasn't in love with her and she was not in love with him, but love had nothing to do with it. He would marry her. She had him neatly trapped.

Her happiness lasted until she was in the apartment. She flicked on the living room light, threw herself down in a comfortable chair, and opened her purse to check her appearance in her compact.

Then she knew he would never marry her. He would very probably never see her again.

The swine, she thought. The dirty rotten no-good miserable swine.

The snake. The louse, the rat.

The bastard.

He had placed three crisp, fresh, brand-new hundred-dollar bills in her purse.

Chapter Eight

TO HELL WITH Sunday.

Sunday was a day during which Joan McKay returned to the apartment at nine in the morning and curled up with Cornwall Becke's thin volume of verse. Because she got home before anybody else woke up, no explanations were in order. For all they knew, she had been home all night.

She did not tell them otherwise. She stayed in her room for the bulk of the day, spending half her time with Cornwall Becke's poems and the other half of her time with her own private thoughts. She was busy getting herself adjusted to the idea of sleeping with a man. When one is not only a virgin but also a lesbian, this takes a little adjusting.

Sunday was a day during which Joe Jeffers and Marilyn Harper tried mightily to forget that they had a problem. Neither one discussed the whole topic of marriage. They concentrated instead on having a good time on Joe's last day in New York. His plane left Idlewild early Monday morning—thus it was their last day together, and for all they knew it would be the last time they would ever see each other.

So they tried to have fun.

They walked over to Central Park, then took a leisurely stroll all the way across to the small zoo on the west side of the park. They looked at animals and wandered around holding hands like high school sweethearts. They sat on a bench and even necked a little.

They went to an off-Broadway play—Broadway closes on Sundays—and they enjoyed it. They returned to the apartment and made love. She knew he would be gone in the morning.

Sunday was a day during which Saundra Stone seriously considered slashing her wrists. As far as she was concerned, everything possible had gone wrong. And it wasn't even Johnny's fault—much as she wanted to blame the son of a bitch, the blame wouldn't stick to him. He'd probably thought she expected the money. As far as he was concerned, she was an urchin way below his social class who was fun in the hay but good for nothing more. After her attempt to ingratiate herself, he had paid her off and dismissed her.

At least she'd gotten three hundred dollars out of the deal. Maybe it was better that way, she thought. She'd given out enough free samples in her day. Maybe she ought to go whole-hog and put it on a paying basis.

Sure.

So she spent the day moping around the apartment, boring herself stiff in front of the television set, alternately pitying herself and despising herself.

That was Sunday.

As stated not long ago, to hell with Sunday.

THE ALARM WOKE Marilyn at a quarter to eight on Monday morning. Alarms have a habit of doing unpleasant things like that. She sat bolt upright in bed before opening her eyes. Then she looked around, blinked unhappily, and glared at the clock. It was still ringing mercilessly.

She walked over to where it jangled and pressed the button that silenced its metallic voice. Only then, when she turned and looked at the bed, did she realize that Joe was gone. The bed looked incredibly empty. The whole room felt empty, simply because he was not there with her.

She mentally contrasted that moment to a similar moment two days ago when she had awakened to find him asleep beside her. Then, strangely enough, she'd been annoyed with him for being there.

Now she was sorry he was gone.

She managed to beat Sandstone to the shower. While the water poured down upon her she tried to get herself into the proper Monday morning mood. Marilyn was one of the few persons in the entire country, if not the world, who did not despise Monday mornings. As a matter of fact, she rather liked Monday mornings. It was never a chore for her to get back into the saddle after a weekend of controlled dissipation. She used the weekend to unwind the tensions of the previous week, and after the weekend had loosened her up, she liked nothing better than to hop back once more into harness and turn her energies to solving the problems which confronted Phulcorte Press.

Her breathless anticipation this morning was not up to par. She dried off after her shower, dressed, made coffee and scrambled a pair of eggs. She polished off breakfast in short order while Sandstone was still contending with her single cup of jet black coffee. Then, briefcase in hand, she headed for the office.

There was a gratifyingly large amount of work waiting for her. Scripts to read, an agent to talk with, an appointment with a writer. She worked non-stop until noon, started to go out for lunch, then changed her mind suddenly and called out for a sandwich and a container of coffee. The sandwich was skimpy and the coffee had that cardboard taste which all coffee has when served in a cardboard cup, but she ate the sandwich and drank the coffee and lit another cigarette while she turned her attention to the work of the day.

She dialed a number.

"Al? This is Marilyn Harper over at Phulcorte. We like the Cannon confession. I'm putting through a voucher for it. Has he done any more? Send some over—we like the way he writes. But that's not what I called about . . . that's right, the Hoban script. It's not bad, Al, but he hasn't got our slant at all. I realize it wasn't done specifically for us, I'm not knocking the piece, it's good. If he could rewrite it I'd like another look at it. It'll have to be on spec, Al. I can't promise. But we pay good rates, and I think it would be worth his while. Fine. I'll hold the script for a pick-up."

She cradled the phone, picked up another script and started to read it. The first and second readers had passed it on to her and she studied it carefully. A confession story, sin and suffer and repent. It was the old saw about the girl who had to choose between love and a job, and—

And she recognized herself.

And shuddered.

My God, she thought, am I *that* trite? Am I just another cliche from every cruddy piece of pulp fiction since the beginning of time? Is that all I am?

She did not finish the story. Instead she took a sheet of her memo paper from her top drawer, scrawled *Rejected . . . too trite . . . MH* on it, and flipped it into her OUT box. She would not buy that story. She would not even read it.

The pressure held up throughout the day, but somehow her enthusiasm for her work was not as high as it had generally been in the past. It was natural, she told herself. She was emotionally upset—she'd made the mistake of getting involved with a man on more than a purely physical level, and cutting the strings of her attachment was certainly not going to be painless. But things would be better. In another day or two, or a week at the outside, Joe Jeffers would be little more than a memory. She would not forget him—why forget a pleasant experience?—but she would cease to think so often about him. And what might or might not be love would pass away soon enough.

Suddenly she wondered what he was doing. His plane must have arrived in Kansas City around the time she was eating breakfast. He'd go home, change his clothes, probably shower. He was remarkably neat for a man.

Then to work. To the main store, probably. She wondered how the stores looked, what they were like. He seemed to have quite a thriving business. Probably made lot of money.

She wondered what his house looked like. He still had the house, hadn't given it up when his wife died. She wondered what kind of a car he drove, if he was a good driver or not. He probably was, she decided. He did everything else well. He was such a thoroughly competent man.

She decided that she was thinking altogether too much about Joe Jeffers.

She looked down at the memo pad on her desk. She had been doodling unconsciously.

She had written *Marilyn Jeffers*.

She stared. What the hell was happening to her? It was ridiculous, frightening.

God!

She ripped off the sheet of paper, tore it into a dozen scraps of paper, crumpled the scraps and put them into the wastebasket beside her desk.

God!

She took a deep breath. Easy, she thought. Everything was going to be all right. All she had to do was pour her heart and soul into the job. Work was the cure-all. Work would push the man from her mind. Work would do the trick.

Work was not working.

The hours dragged by, and she wondered what in God's name she was going to do.

"I HAVE A proposition for you," Joan McKay said.

Harvey Chase looked up. His eyes were still bloodshot from the weekend. He looked unhappy.

"Let's have it."

Joan took a deep breath. She was remarkably unsure of herself, more so than ever before. It would not be at all easy to get herself boffed by a man. She didn't know how to go about it, exactly. It was something she had never done before.

She had picked the man, however. Harvey Chase seemed to be the obvious choice. Not unattractive. A man she knew and liked. A good point to start with.

But now what did she do? She couldn't lie down on the floor with her skirt hiked over her knees and her panties down around her ankles. She couldn't grin and say *Make love to me, sweets.*

This would not work.

Nor could she tell him the truth. *I'm a lesbian, Harv old kid. I want to straighten out. Make love to me so that I'll know what it's all about. Just a quickie. I've never been made love to, you see, and I want to see what I'm missing. But be gentle, dammit, because I'm scared stiff.*

That would not be the right approach.

"Tonight," she said, trying to keep it light, "you will buy me a dinner. A good dinner. Not necessarily an expensive dinner, but a good one. With a drink or two and maybe a little wine. It won't cost you anything. You can charge it to *Agony* as a business expense. Every editor wines and dines his secretary at one point or another. It's protocol."

He stared at her. "You broke?"

"No."

"Then what's the bit?"

"I want to have dinner with you."

"Yeah?"

She nodded solemnly.

"Hmmmm," he said. He studied her and she flushed a little under his gaze.

"Dinner," he said thoughtfully.

"That's right."

"And then what?"

"I don't know," she said.

"Oh," he said.

She did not say anything now. She had laid it on the line about as neatly as anyone possibly could, and he had gotten the message. She wasn't sure whether she had done a good job or not. Probably not, she decided. She'd probably been too brazen, too bold.

"Sounds like a good idea," he said. "Sounds like a hell of a good idea. I should have taken you out to dinner long ago, little girl. An error of omission."

"But easily corrected."

"True."

He smiled briefly, then returned to the work on his desk. She was glad of that. He could have made the evening markedly unpleasant, simply by pushing things before it was time. He knew and she knew that they were going to sleep together. But, by pushing this fact away for the duration of the afternoon, he had done her a great favor. It made things simpler.

She reread the poem on the desk.

You see a pattern in the morning groan
When the young sun womb-bursts with a flushed red face
And fills the diaper sky. Your sterile soul
Begs for banalities to call its own
And holds forth withered breasts. In the first place
When you have seen sufficient suns you'll know
They're all the same; each one is round and whole
And bright, and vomits blood on scabrous skies.
Thirst for your tepid milk? I tried it once
And promptly spat it out. It's black as coal
Sunrise leaves fools and fairies short of breath;
And tastes of underarms and powdered bone.
And sunset's just as deadly dull as death.

She reread it. It was as powerfully savage a poem as she had read in a long while and she was unsure how to react to it. She shook her head.

"Harvey? Want to take a look at this?"

He took the poem from her.

"'Rapture At Dawning,'" he intoned solemnly, "By Lance Brecklow. Phony-sounding name."

"Just read it."

He read it. He looked up, a bit disturbed, and stared at her. "This Brecklow fellow," he said, "is an unhappy man. Most unpleasant poem I've ever read."

"I know."

"Like it?"

"Not particularly," she said.

"Well—"

"I don't think you're supposed to like it," she said. "It's supposed to revolt you."

"We should publish revolting poetry?"

"If it's good."

He sighed. "It lives up to the magazine's name, anyway. The most agonizing piece of poetry in a while. I'll think about it, read it over."

He put it in the MAYBE basket and turned back to his work. She opened another envelope and started reading. This was good, she thought. This was the way it ought to be. Not a casual encounter between two total strangers but an affair—or at least an attempt at an affair—between a man and woman who enjoyed a certain amount of friendship coupled with a certain amount of professional closeness to begin with.

She hoped it would work out. She did not want to be a lesbian. If a heterosexual relationship was only half as physically enjoyable as a homosexual one, she would still prefer it. It was easily worth that much to her to be normal.

Whatever normal meant.

At five o'clock Harvey Chase groaned mightily, swept papers off his desk and into the desk's top drawer, and closed the drawer. "Let's go," he said. "Mondays aren't meant for work. They're strictly for purposes of recuperation. Let's go somewhere and recuperate."

"A sound idea."

"C'mon," he said, slipping into his tweed jacket. "Away from the agony of *Agony*. Away from the hordes of Lance Brecklows and multitudes of *As the Twig is Bent's*. Away from all this nonsense. I'm starving."

"Me too."

"Onward!"

And away they went. They walked down the three flights of stairs and out onto the street. It was warm—muggy and dull, the air still, the streets crowded with cars and pedestrians. They headed south on University Place then cut west and south again to a small restaurant on Sullivan Street. The place was called Dolor de Estomago, a picturesque phrase meaning *stomach ache* in Spanish. Malaga bottles with candles dripping on them sat in the middle of red checkerboard table cloths. The food was Spanish, and cheap, and good.

They had the paella. They drank a good bottle of Malaga. They made very small talk.

Joan McKay was both frightened and happy. She talked easily and smiled freely and tried to cover her fear. Soon they would leave the restaurant. Soon they would go to Harvey's apartment. Soon the Vestal Virgin would open her portals to admit a man to her private chamber.

Soon.

And she prayed to Allah and Vishnu and Buddha that it would work out.

THE PHONE WAS ringing when Saundra Stone walked into the apartment on 73rd Street. She wanted very much to let it ring. It had been one hell of a dull day at work, and she was heartily damned sick of Caution Insurance and their typewriter which she had been so diligently and so unwillingly pounding, and she had a splitting headache, and she did not want to talk to anyone on the telephone.

But it was ringing. And the jangling ring-ring-ring of the rotten phone was not helping her head at all.

So she answered it.

It was Frank Ralston. "This is Frank, Sandstone. I tried to get you all weekend but nobody answered. What's new?"

"Very little."

"Today was a hell of a day," he said. "Work, work, work. I hate work, Sandstone."

There were times for small talk, and there were other times. This was one of the other times. She thought of hanging up on him but decided against it. It wouldn't work. The jerk would think they'd been disconnected and would call back again.

Of course, she could always hang up again. In time he would get the message. But it would take too long, and in the meanwhile there would be the jangling of the phone, and this she could not take.

"What did you want?"

"Just your company," he said. "Busy tonight?"

"Yes," she lied. "I'm sorry," she lied.

"Tomorrow night?"

"Well—"

"Dinner," he said. "I'll buy you a good dinner. How does that sound?"

Wonderful it didn't sound. But she knew instinctively that if she told him she'd be busy Tuesday night, he'd ask her how about Wednesday, and in time she'd be unable to invent even an implausible excuse.

"It sounds wonderful," she said.

"Pick you up sixish?"

"Fine."

"Swell," he said. "I'll wear my Brooks Brother suit. That shows how fond I am of you."

And, happily, he hung up.

Sandstone sat down heavily and tried to relax, which was easier said than done. She wandered into the bathroom, juggled three aspirin, popped them into her mouth and drowned them with a glass of water. Aspirin never helped. She knew this, but if she didn't take them she would sit around thinking *I really ought to take an aspirin or two or three*, and that made it even worse. So she took three aspirin whenever she had a headache, which was often, and they never did any good at all.

What the hell.

She thought about cooking dinner. That, she decided, would not be too bad. But after she cooked it she would have to eat it, and that would be horrible.

So to hell with cooking dinner.

She was still busy trying to adjust to the fun and games with Johnny Lipton. The affair called for an agonizing reappraisal of her foreign policy. It seemed evident to her that she was not going to marry Johnny Lipton. Nor was she going to marry *any* really rich man, by the looks of things.

It just wasn't working out.

Which meant she had to decide what she wanted. She could marry Frank Ralston, she felt certain. It would not be difficult. She had an advantage already—he was chasing her and she was running away from him. All she had to do was slow down a bit and let him catch her.

Simple.

Very simple,

Eminently simple.

But did she *want* Frank Ralston?

Now there was a question. A hell of a good question. If you added it all up on paper, it made relatively good sense to take a crack at Frank Ralston. He was already more or less in love with her, or would be if she gave him the least bit of encouragement. And he was good in bed—not something incredible like Johnny Lipton, but good. More than good, even.

So?

And he was also making a living, and would make a better living in time, and while he would never become rich, he would give her a home and a family and a certain measure of security. Her parents would approve of him, not that it mattered to her, and his parents would approve of her, not that it probably mattered to him, and that would be that.

So?

But she didn't love Frank Ralston.

Well, hell, she told herself, you don't love Johnny Lipton and you were pretty hot to marry him. Which turned out to be pretty much out of the question. So why should love enter into the picture with Frank?

A good question.

He wasn't bad, she decided. A little too fey maybe, with *Let's run it up the flagpole and see who salutes* and other Ulcer Gulch witticisms. But it could be worse. She could imagine the conversation already when the real rock-bottom hard-core dialogue of Madison Avenue became a part of his speech:

"Say, Sandypoo, why don't we knock off a little piecerino? Just a quickie-poo."

Uh-huh.

That was all she needed.

But she was not being fair. He pwas a solid-citizen middle-class type, to be sure. But she was more or less the same thing. Why should she put on airs?

Another good question.

And she suddenly wished Marilyn would get back to the

apartment. She could talk this over with Marilyn, get her opinion. Marilyn was a good sounding board; she'd nipped more than a few of Sandstone's stupidities in the bud.

She sighed. Her head was splitting. If the aspirin had been any help, she couldn't figure out what they had done for her. Maybe the best headache remedy was decapitation.

Or the loss of a job. Her job was a first-class headache, dammit. If nothing else, marriage to Frank would remove her once and for all from the ranks of the employed. That was something. She wondered idly how many girls had gotten married solely to cease working. A lot, she would bet. A hell of a lot.

DINNER WAS OVER.

Harvey Chase called for the check and paid for it. They stood up and he led the way out of Dolor de Estomago. Happily, Joan did not have a stomach ache. She was glad of this. The picture of losing one's virginity while in the grip of a fierce intestinal pain was not a pretty one.

"Well," he said. "Where to?"

"Anywhere."

He smiled. "I don't have any etchings," he said, "but I've been doing some writing. Like to come up and take a look?"

"Think it's safe?"

"Safe as the first national."

"Okay. What are you working on?"

"Novel," he said. They headed north and west in the general direction of his apartment, which was on Christopher Street the other side of Seventh Avenue. "Just a novel," he went on, several minutes later. "Not a very good one, I'm afraid. It's crawling along. I don't know where exactly it's headed."

"First novel?"

He nodded. "That's the trouble. Novels are deceptively simple. Nice and loose—you just keep writing and let the book move along. Except you don't go anywhere. I'm fifty pages in already and I'll be damned if I know what should happen next. My characters are wobbly and if there's a plot I don't know about it."

His apartment was on the second floor of a small, attractive brownstone on Christopher Street. It was neat and sloppy at once—a very bachelorish place. Everything had a place and was in it but at the same time the floor was unswept, the walls dirty, the ashtrays overflowing.

There was just one room and a kitchenette. The bed, while only partially made, was clean. She approved of that. She only hoped she wouldn't mess his sheets too much.

A portable typewriter rested on a bridge table with piles of manuscripts on either side. "The novel," he said, walking toward the table.

"Later."

He turned to her.

"I'll read the novel," she promised. "I want to read it. I'll read it . . . afterwards."

He smiled. He walked to her and his arms went around her

and she melted against him, hoping against hope that it would work, that he would be strong enough and good enough to make it all right for her.

He kissed her. She stiffened momentarily—it was involuntary; she couldn't help it. Then she forced herself to relax, forced herself to respond to his kiss.

It wasn't bad. It wasn't good, but it wasn't bad either.

"Be gentle," she said. "Be gentle with me. I—"

He kissed her again, and almost before she realized it she was lying on his bed. He hovered over her, his mouth glued to hers, and she tried desperately to feel some positive emotion, some physical excitement, when his tongue stole between her lips and into her mouth.

She felt nothing.

Nothing at all.

She lay there, almost inert, while he undressed first her and then himself. The touch of his bare body against hers sent a little shiver through her, and when he began to handle her breasts, his hands a bit clumsy and yet strangely sure of themselves, she began to respond. It wasn't phony, it wasn't forced—it was real, and her heart sang.

He kissed her.

Touched her.

Caressed her.

Her excitement began to mount and she thought that it was okay now, that everything was going to be all right, that she had nothing to worry about. He kept working on her, touching and kissing and caressing, and she knew that it was about to begin, that it would begin at any moment now, and she hoped that it wouldn't hurt, that it would be all right.

She felt him pressing against her. She held her breath and waited, wondering what would happen, wondering what it would be like.

And then it happened.

It was pain, sheer pain and nothing but pain. It was a knife thrust through a piece of sheer silk, ripping and tearing, and she screamed out into the night. He was filling her and tearing her apart, and she couldn't help screaming. Any excitement she might have felt had vanished forever the minute he entered her. It was gone, long gone, and its place was taken by the all-consuming pain that coursed through her.

He moved within her, moved quickly, and she closed her eyes and winced through pain.

It kept going on.

Then a quick hot spasm indicated completion on his part. She lay very still while he relaxed, then withdrew from her. Then she turned her face to his pillow and began to cry.

"You should have told me you were a virgin, Joan."

She couldn't answer him. A virgin? She had been more than virgin.

A lesbian.

"Joan?"

She turned to him. Her face was stained with tears and he looked at her, his face troubled.

"There's more to it than that, isn't there? Tell me about it, Joan."

"Nothing to tell."

"Are you sure?"

She looked away.

"I'm a good listener, Joan. Try me."

"I don't want to talk about it."

"You sure?"

Was she sure? Was she sure about anything? How in hell did she know?

"Tell me about it, Joan."

She did not want to tell him. She did not want to speak to anyone, not even herself. She did not want to think or feel, did not want even to exist. She had tried, she had fought to become normal, but nothing had worked for her, nothing at all. She was a lesbian who did not want to be a lesbian, and if there was anything on earth more wretched than that, she did not know what it could be.

She did not want to tell him.

"Joan—"

She stood up, stood up from the bed, and she fumbled for her clothing. He had dropped them to the floor, but she found them in no time at all and began to get dressed. She dressed deliberately but quickly. She ignored him while she dressed, then turned and focused defiantly sad eyes upon him.

"I'll tell you," she said.

He stared at her.

"I'll tell you. I'll even surprise you. What do you know about the girl you just made love to, Harvey?"

"Not very much."

"Do you know that she sleeps with girls?" Her voice rose. "Do you know she's a dirty little dyke? Do you know she's a lesbian? Do you know that, Harvey?"

"Joan—"

She turned away from him and ran for the door. He called after her but she paid no attention to him. He was undressed and he could not follow her.

"Come back, Joan. Come back here, will you? I want to talk to you!"

But she did not want to talk to him. She did not even want to see him. She wanted to be alone.

She ran out of his building and into the night.

Chapter Nine

"NOW LET ME get this straight," Marilyn said.

"Let's take it from the top, as the young-men-in-a-hurry might phrase it. You've got a problem."

"Right," Saundra said.

"All of a sudden you're not trying to marry a rich man," Marilyn went on. "You won't tell me why, but it's probably something that happened with that Lipton character. Don't worry—I won't pry. You've got your reasons. I'll accept them blind. Isn't that remarkably nice of me?"

"Uh-huh."

"So let's get to the point. Frank Wheaties called you to-night and—"

"Ralston."

"Whatever. He called you and asked you out for—tomor-row night. And you're going out with him. And you think he'll get around to marriage in no time at all if you give him half a chance. That's the bit, huh?"

"Uh-huh."

"But you don't love him."

Saundra shrugged.

"And you don't know whether or not you want to marry him."

She nodded.

"So what am I supposed to tell you? Hell, I can't give advice to the lovelorn. I'm past the earnest helpmate stage. I've got problems of my own, baby. I don't have the world by the tail any more. I used to think I did. Now I'm not so sure. I should tell you to marry this goof? I can't even run my own life straight, Sandstone. I've been going nuts all day long, I'm starting to feel like a true-confessions character, it's a pain in the neck. What can I tell you? I don't know."

"Joe?"

"Joe."

"You miss the guy."

"Yeah," she said. "Yeah, I miss the guy. That sort of sums it up, doesn't it? I miss the guy."

"Well—"

"Well. I miss the guy, and if I had half a brain I'd get on the next plane out of here, and I don't have half a brain, and God alone knows what I'm going to do next. So here we are. And you want me to tell you what to do? You must be out of your mind."

Sandstone sighed. "Thanks for nothing," she said. "No use talking to you, I guess. Maybe I should ask the Vestal Virgin. She might have a word of wisdom."

"Is she home?"

Saundra shook her head. "Out. Out almost all the time, it

seems to me. At any rate, she's out whenever I'm home. Which isn't too goddamned often, come to think of it. If she's home whenever I'm out, then she's home almost all the time."

"Huh?"

"I'm not too sure myself what I said. The hell with it. She's out, huh?"

"Looks that way."

"I really don't understand that girl," Saundra said. "She keeps so much of herself hidden. I hardly know her anymore. Know what I mean?"

Marilyn nodded. "A tenth of her is showing. The other nine-tenths stays below the surface."

"Like an iceberg?"

"Sort of."

"Well, hell. She's always been like an iceberg, when you stop to think about it."

"Don't be so sure."

"Huh?"

"Just a feeling I've got," Marilyn said. "A hunch. I don't think the Vestal Virgin is a virgin anymore."

THE VESTAL VIRGIN was not a virgin any more.

She was sitting in Dragonet, a small coffee house on the east side of the Village. Periodically she took a bitter sip of espresso coffee from the demitasse cup on the small table before her. Periodically she read a paragraph of the book she was holding. It was a paperback mystery novel, a sex-and-sadism synopticon which was not holding her interest at all. She'd picked it up from a table in front of a used book store on Fourth Street for a dime, wanting something to read, but now she didn't want to read any more.

There was nothing she wanted to do.

She glanced around the small shop. Dragonet was not a homosexual hangout—the clientele was composed mostly of young artists and students who spent their time in the Village and drank coffee because they could not afford anything stronger. The coffee house was a place where she could be alone to think her own private thoughts, alone but not isolated, alone but with people around her. It was what she needed.

She was very unhappy.

Wretched, perhaps, is a more accurate word. Joan McKay was wretched. The best-laid plans of mice and men gang aft aglay, and now, although both her plans and she had been best-laid, she was about as aglay as you could get.

Which is to say that she was still Joan McKay, girl lesbian, and quite miserable about the whole thing.

She sipped her coffee.

I could try again, she thought hysterically. I could try again and next time the pain wouldn't be so bad, and maybe I would get to like it. It was just the pain, that was the only thing that was wrong, just the damned pain. I was even beginning to enjoy it before all that pain. Maybe—

But that wasn't it. Because she had a feeling that the pain had been more mental than physical, more fear and tension than the ripping and tearing of tender flesh. The pain was gone now, long gone, but the memory of pain and fear and tension and everything else was still with her. It would be with her forever.

She wanted to cry.

She took another sip of her coffee. Then she picked up the paperback mystery novel, the synopticon of sex and sadism, and began to read. The book was written in the first person, narrated by the semiliterate detective:

She had the kind of body you wanted to reach out and grab hold of. Big blossoming breasts that peered out at me through the top of the peasant blouse. Hips that were trying to tear her skirt apart. Legs like pistons.

"I have to see you," she said. "It's important."

I didn't care whether it was important or not. I just wanted to take those big breasts in my hands and squeeze them until she went limp. I took a step toward her . . .

Joan closed the book. She put it down on the top of the small table and looked up. She almost jumped out of her seat. There was a man sitting across the table from her.

"Good book?"

He had a broad forehead and deep dark eyes. His beard was full and dark brown, just a shade lighter than his hair. He was wearing a plaid wool shirt and a pair of Levi's. He was thirty, she guessed. Maybe older, maybe younger. The beard hid his age.

"You looked lonely," he said. "Very lonely. Pretty girls shouldn't waste their time with stupid books."

"They shouldn't?"

"Of course not."

"What should they do?"

"They should spend their time with men," the man with the beard said. "Men who can take care of them."

"Like you?"

"Like me."

His confidence was at once disquieting and calming, a strange paradox. He was easily the most self-confident man she had ever met. There was not a shadow of doubt in his approach. His eyes were bold and she had trouble meeting them. She could not help feeling that he knew everything there was to know about her, that he could just look at her for a few minutes and know the entire story of her life.

"What do you want?"

"You."

"Me?"

"You," he said.

She didn't say anything. She wanted to get up and run. She wanted to scream.

She stayed where she was and looked at him, at his eyes, and she was afraid. She did not know what was going to happen next. She did not want to think about it.

"What do you do?"

"Nothing," he said.

"How do you . . . earn a living?"

He shrugged. "Money is easy to get," he said. "I get what I need. I live."

She had never met anyone like him.

"I've got a place," he said. "A loft on East Fifth Street. A dump but livable. We're going to go there, you and me. Now. I'm going to take your clothes off and toss you on the bed. Then we'll roll around for an hour or so. Let's move."

She did not want to go. If there was one thing she was not looking forward to, it was an hour or so of rolling around with this bearded lunatic. She was afraid of him. He looked incredibly strong, as though he could tear her head from her body with one hand.

There would be pain. More pain than before, and less pleasure, and more disappointment. She wanted to go back to her own apartment, to the safety of solitude, to her own little bed. But she knew that this was out of the question. He wanted her to come with him. She had no choice in the matter. If he wanted her, now, she would go to him. There was absolutely nothing else she could do.

She stood up.

"C'mon."

"I have to pay for the—"

"Forget it. They can afford it."

"But—"

"C'mon."

They walked out of Dragonet and nobody asked her for

the money for the espresso. She wondered whether they didn't notice or if they, too, were afraid of him.

It was cool out, now. He was holding onto her arm, leading her south and east toward his apartment. He did not speak, and she had nothing to say, so they walked on in silence.

It was incredible. She had been a virgin for so many years, so damned many years, and now she was going to make love to two men in the space of one evening. She had already been made love to by one man—Harvey Chase.

It had been bad.

Now this man, whose name she did not and probably would never know, was going to repeat the process. She knew in advance that it was going to be bad, that she would not enjoy it at all. But there was nothing she could do about it. She had to go through with it, no matter how unpleasant it was.

There was no way out.

He lived on the third floor of a run-down five-story tenement. The hallways smelled of people and stale cabbage. The paint was peeling from the walls. The stairs squeaked.

His door was unlocked. He shoved it open and led her into his apartment. It was a mess—one broken-down bed that sagged in the middle, one cane-bottomed chair, one chest of drawers scarred by the butts of a thousand forgotten cigarettes. The floor was piled high with garbage and discarded clothing. She heard something that sounded like a mouse squealing. She saw roaches racing in single file over one wall.

She shuddered.

"Strip," he told her. "Peel."

She removed her clothing.

"The bed."

She lay down.

She did as she was told.

Then it began.

It was not good, but it was not painful. This surprised her. She thought that any love play with a man would perforce be painful to her. This was not the case. The pain that had been present with Harvey was gone now. But nothing took its place, nothing at all.

She felt nothing.

It was very strange. Her body remained on the sagging bed, remained in the embrace of the bearded man. But her mind was somewhere else entirely, a mind divorced from its body and floating free in space and time. Her body submitted to him, even went through the motions of response.

Her brain stayed alone. She saw and heard and felt nothing, nothing at all.

Then, at last, it was over. It was good for him, as she could see. He moved faster and faster, and then he went very tense.

Then he moved away from her and lay on his side, breathing heavily for several minutes.

Then he rolled onto his stomach.

"Get dressed," he told her. "You got what you came for. Now scram. Put your clothes on and get out."

Rude, she thought. Not gentlemanly at all.

She got dressed, quickly, and she left his apartment. She walked down the stairs and smelled the smells of people and stale cabbage. In the front hallway a leather-jacketed boy was embracing a busty, sweatered girl. They didn't seem to notice her. She walked past them, followed Fifth Street to the first wide avenue with taxis cruising, hailed a cab and sank back into her seat, exhausted and numb.

Twice.

Two men in one night.

And now she did not have to try any longer. She had tried with Harvey Chase, tried and failed. And she had permitted the bearded man to use her body, but by then she was not even trying because she knew that it would not work. The game was over. She was what she was—period. End of report.

Now she had her life to live. It was not the life she had wanted. Not the life of a normal woman, with husband and home and children. That would not be her life. It was a pretty pattern, but it was not a pattern into which she could fit herself.

She fit another pattern.

A pattern that drifted in the shadows. A gay pattern, a lesbian pattern.

Wafting shadows . . .

"This right, lady?"

The cab was in front of her building now. She told the driver this was fine, perfect, and thank you very much. She paid him and tipped him and got out of the cab. She walked into the building, rode the elevator to her floor, went into her apartment.

The die was cast now, the Rubicon crossed. Everything was set, everything determined. She was Joan McKay, the lesbian. That was the way the ball bounced.

It could be worse, she thought. It could be a great deal worse. At least she knew for certain who she was and what she was. There would be no more pretending. With certain knowledge came acceptance. The guilt feelings would vanish. She would live her life, fully and properly, and everything would be all right.

"Well," Sandstone said to her. "If it isn't the Vestal Virgin. How's virginity?"

Joan McKay smiled.

MONDAY HAD BEEN bad enough. Monday, with its confession stories with which she identified. Monday, with its oppressive routine and its overwhelming boredom.

Monday had been miserable.

Well, Tuesday was worse.

Marilyn Harper sat at her desk and watched the clock. She had hardly ever done this before. Marilyn Harper was not a clock-watcher. The little featherheads who wasted time in the typing pool and waited for a man to come and marry them, impregnate them, and hustle them off to Levittown—they watched the clock. Not Marilyn. She was hard working. She was a dedicated employee, anxious to get ahead. She did not clock-watch.

Now she was watching the clock. The big hand was on the ten, and the little hand was edging toward the five, and in ten minutes the big hand would be on the twelve and the little hand would have reached the five. It would be five o'clock, and end of another day of work at Phulcorte Press, and Marilyn Harper would clear off her desk and head for home.

She stared at the clock.

God, it had been a day. Too much work and too much aggravation and too much irritation and too much nonsense and, oh, just too damned much of everything. Her head ached—not painfully, just dully, a steady throb that she could not totally ignore. And her behind ached from the eight—count 'em, eight—precious hours she'd spent sitting in the damned chair.

A horrible day.

And what was really annoying was the fact that the day had not been different from all the others she had spent on the job. It was pretty much the same—the same things to read, the same agents to call, the same everything to do.

Then why was it so horrible?

Answer: It was horrible because she was discovering for the first time that Joe Jeffers, God bless him, was right. She just did not like her job.

A hell of a revelation.

But true, as far as she could see. Before Joe, before a weekend of happiness, a weekend that seemed to have had quite an effect on her young life, she had been content. The job was a means to an end, the end was years in the future, and she could work hard secure in the knowledge that she was working toward a definite goal, a certain aim.

This was no longer the case.

Now it was different. Now the goal seemed farther away than ever, which in itself was not so bad. What was bad was the fact that the goal no longer seemed so mouth-wateringly desirable. Who needed forty grand a year if it meant loneliness and boredom? Who needed to grow old all alone?

Not her.

Not Marilyn Harper.

And she missed him, that was the hell of it. She would sit at her desk and hold imaginary conversations with him, and this was certainly not designed to improve her disposition. She would wonder what he was doing, what clothes he was wearing, whether he was sitting or standing or lying down. And, more important, she would wonder what he was thinking about. Was he remembering her? Was she on his mind?

Or had he forgotten her already?

That was possible. For all she knew she was just a casual weekend romance, just an affectionate roll in warm sweet-smelling hay, just a handy thing to take to bed in the big city before returning to Kay Cee.

She did not believe this.

If she had been able to believe this, if she could feel certain that she meant nothing to him, then he would cease to mean something to her. But she knew with awesome certainty that he wanted her, that he liked her, that he . . . yes, loved her.

This changed things.

This kept her mind hopping all over the damned place, kept her from settling down and relaxing.

Kept her eyes on the clock.

Then, all at once, it was five. She cleared off her desk like a mindless robot, tucked briefcase under her arm and headed out of the office. She said goodbyes to people, rode the elevator to the lobby, and left the building.

What next?

She most definitely did not feel like returning to the apartment. She didn't want to cook, and she didn't want to be alone in the apartment. She didn't even relish the notion of the ride back to the place, whether it was via bus or subway or taxi. Dinner out was a far superior idea.

Yes.

She had roast pork and Chinese vegetables in the Haow Naow, a medium-priced Chinese restaurant on West 47th Street. She broke open her fortune cookie and discovered that she was going to meet a dark-haired stranger. She crumpled the little slip of rice-paper, ate the cookie, paid the check, tipped the waiter, left the small restaurant.

What next?

She went to a movie and tried to relax and failed. Her mind would not stay on the movie. It stayed instead on Joe Jeffers. This was not good.

Not good at all.

It's just sex, she thought suddenly. He's a man, I need a

man, and if I have a man I'll drive him out of my mind. Sex as therapy. A quickie to get the taste of him out of my mouth. Brush your teeth with a man.

Why not?

She left the theater before the picture ended. She walked a block and found out that she was standing on the sidewalk in front of the Astor Bar. That was where she had met Joe. How long ago was that? Just Friday night. Not long ago at all. Why did it *seem* so long ago? Why did she think or feel or whatever that she and Joe had known each other for years?

Why?

She went inside the bar, took a stool at the bar, ordered a dry Gibson. The drink came, crisp and clear and cool, and she sipped it. A man came up and sat down next to her.

She looked at him and decided that he would do. Tall and slender. Good looking, or at least passable. Well dressed. Out-of-towner, by the looks of things.

Maybe he came from Kansas City. Maybe he knew Joe. Maybe—

"Do you have a match?"

She asked him this, a cigarette between the second and third fingers of her right hand, her eyes properly downcast. She was good at this sort of thing. You had an itch and you scratched it. Why was she so damned itchy all the time?

He took out a lighter and lit her cigarette.

"Nice night out," he said.

She agreed that it was indeed a nice night.

"Just got into town," he said. "Up from Louisville for the furniture dealers convention. Name's Stan Taylor."

She smiled pleasantly.

"Say," he said, his voice easy, "no sense sitting here paying bar prices for liquor. I've got a good bottle up in my room. Why not come on up and have a drink with me?"

She started to agree. But somehow, some why, something within her snapped. It was no good—the fast approach, the quick hunger of two humans itching for sex. All pick-ups were not Joe Jeffers. All men were not what she needed.

"No," she said. "No, I—"

"Awww, come on," he said. "I'm a nice guy. Easy to get along with. We'll have a little party, huh? Just you and me. A few drinks and a good time. I'm a sporting fellow."

"I'm sure you are," she said. "Really, I just stopped for a drink. I have to go home now. I'm sorry."

"How much, sister?"

She stared at him.

"So I made a mistake," he said. "So it's not free. I told you I'm a sport. How much will it cost me to get into you? If the price is right—"

He didn't get to finish that sentence because she slapped him. She slapped hard, putting all her weight into the blow. The sound of the slap echoed throughout the plush interior of the Astor Bar. The patrons, however, were a well-bred lot. Nobody turned to stare. Everybody ignored them.

"Now you listen," she said. Her voice was ice. "You just

listen. You are going to leave me alone, and you are going to stay away from me, or so help me God I am going to kill you."

She turned on her heel and left the bar.

All men were not Joe Jeffers. All pick-ups were not the answer. She shouldn't have slapped him. It was her fault, not his. He'd just put two and two together.

She went home and cried.

THEY WOUND UP, inevitably, at Frank's apartment on West 69th Street.

Saundra Stone had known they would wind up there. It was a foregone conclusion from the minute she agreed to go out with him that evening, at least as far as she was concerned. First a good dinner, then a show, then back to his apartment for a nightcap, an intriguing euphemism if there ever was one. What else?

He was telling her his troubles now. He had a great many troubles, at least according to him, and he was not the sort who liked to keep his troubles to himself. Instead he was telling them to her, and they were boring her silly. If there was one thing she did not feel like doing, it was listening to the trials and tribulations of an ad man.

Was this the man she was going to marry?

Something suddenly struck home. If she married Frank Ralston, she would spend the rest of her life listening to his problems. If she married *anybody*, for that matter, she would spend the rest of her life as a listener, a shoulder to cry on, a helpmate in time of trouble.

She did not want that role. She did not want anybody depending upon her. Not now, not ever. She did not want a houseful of children with running noses, and she did not want a husband with a bleeding ulcer.

She wanted to be on her own.

She had never realized this before. Now, however, she knew it for a fact. She could not go through life as somebody's wife. She had to be alone, to live alone, to think and feel alone.

No other life would suit her.

"Frank," she said suddenly, "you don't want to talk to me. Maybe you want to talk, all right, but not to me."

He looked at her. It was obvious to her that he did not have the faintest idea what she was talking about. Well, she would let him figure it out. She would explain it, bit by bit until he got the full picture. She would run it up the flagpole and see if anybody saluted.

To coin a phrase.

"You don't want to talk to me," she went on. "I'm not the sort of person people talk to. You know what kind of person I am, deep down inside where it counts?"

He looked blank. No, he didn't know what sort of person she was. But she knew. And Johnny Lipton had known, bless him or damn him, as you please. He was a clever fellow, that Johnny Lipton. He knew more about her than she had known. She knew now, of course. He had shown her.

"I'm the sort of person men want to sleep with," she told Frank Ralston. "And, when you boil it down, that's what you want to do. You don't want to talk to me. You want to sleep with me. Isn't that right?"

"Well—"

"Don't you want to sleep with me?"

He was having troubles. He couldn't say *No, I don't want to sleep with you.* That would be a lie, for one thing, and it would defeat his chances of getting her on the rack, for another. But he couldn't tell her point-blank that he *did* want to sleep with her without looking like a monumental clown.

So, wisely enough, he didn't say anything.

Well, he didn't have to. She could do the talking, lay it on the line. He could just sit there and listen to her. That was fine with her. "You want to sleep with me," she said. "Well, that's nothing new. Lots of men want to sleep with me. Lots of them manage it. And I'll be glad to sleep with you, Frank. I really will. I don't want to listen to your troubles, and I don't want to hold out a shoulder for you to cry on, because that's not the sort of girl I am. I want to sleep with you."

"Well," he said.

So she dropped the bomb.

"It'll cost you twenty dollars," she said.

IT TOOK A little while to make him understand what she meant. Well, it was simple enough. She'd been giving it away long enough. Now it was about time she got paid for it. If he wanted her, well, it would cost him. She wasn't going to be an Eighth Avenue whore, wasn't going to take on a hundred men a night to support a junk habit or anything of the sort. She was going to put out, and she was going to get paid.

And was he interested?

Yeah, he was interested.

He was still a little stunned, and it was obvious to her that he didn't get the whole bit yet, but he was interested. He knew damned well she was worth the twenty, and he had twenty to spare, and he wanted her.

That was that.

He gave her the twenty first, and she folded the bill and put it in her purse. Then he turned off the lights and they got undressed. She took off all her clothes and piled them on a chair. Then she lay down on the bed and he joined her.

It was just as good when you got paid, she found out. Just as good. A man's hands felt just the same on your breasts, and a man's mouth tasted just as sweet, and the whole process was no less enjoyable as a result of the fact that you'd earned yourself twenty bucks for the effort.

It was fun.

Genuine fun.

They lay there for quite a time, with her fondling him and with him running his hands over her. Then they were ready, and she stretched out and he came to her. It did not take very long. He was with her and it was very good.

Not the end of the world, but good.

Not as good as with Johnny Lipton, but more than adequate.

Nothing to write home about, but nothing to cry over either.

It was fine. It would have been for free, and it was even better with twenty bucks thrown in.

And then it was over.

He didn't want to talk to her afterwards, for some unfathomable reason, but she didn't particularly give a damn one way or the other. She dressed in a hurry, gave him a quick kiss goodbye and hurried out of the apartment.

She was happy.

Very happy.

She had just discovered a marvelous well-paying career.

Chapter Ten

FLIGHT 504 WAS ONE of the new jets. It made the New York–Los Angeles flight with one stop in the middle of the country at Kansas City. It was a large plane, with a pilot and a co-pilot and two stewardesses.

The pilot's name was Don McAllister. He was tall and very thin, with a long face broken in two by a thick moustache that curled over his upper lip and looked sinister. It was the only thing about his face which did look sinister. He was twenty-eight years old but looked several years younger. His face was pink and healthy-looking. His eyes were light blue.

The co-pilot's name was Leon Gray. He was also twenty-eight years old, strangely enough, and he looked thirty-five. He drank. An occupational disease among flight personnel, and not nearly so dangerous as one might think. Leon Gray did not drink before a flight and he did not drink during a flight. He drank after flights, and on days when he was not scheduled to fly, and he drank like a fish. His eyes were watery and the veins in his face were broken, a road map of broken blood vessels on a face that, like his last name, was gray.

The two stewardesses were easy to tell apart. One was tall

and blonde and the other was short and dark. The tall blonde was named Betty Cameron. She had big breasts and a narrow waist and wide hips, and she was sleeping off and on with Leon Gray. The short brunette was named Anita Hickman. She had small breasts and a narrow waist and slender hips, and she was sleeping off and on with Leon Gray also.

Both of the stewardesses were members of the Mile High Club. A stewardess qualifies for the Mile High Club by getting made love to while her plane is up in the air. This is not as difficult as it sounds. The crews of commercial airlines are made up of astute and resourceful personnel.

Now, however, one may cease to think about Don McAllister and Leon Gray and Betty Cameron and Anita Hickman. If this plane were about to crash, or make a forced landing, or if some joker had a bomb in his suitcase, or something like that, then the members of the crew would be important here. Relax. Everything's all right—the plane will land neatly in Kansas City airport, make a smooth take-off and proceed on schedule to Los Angeles. One can forget the crew. Concentrate instead upon the passenger in the seat nearest to the right wing—

Marilyn Harper's emotions were hard to pin down. She was not happy, exactly, nor was she sad. She was neither afraid nor totally free from fear. She did not even have the feeling of relief one gets from having come to a correct and necessary decision. In point of fact, she had not come upon a decision at all. The decision, such as it was, had been made for her.

She could not remain at her job, not anymore. The job

was over and done with as far as she was concerned. Nor could she ease her tensions with other men—men other than Joe Jeffers, that is. It was not going to work for her with any other man. The man in the Astor Bar for example; his approach had seemed crude and disgusting, but the same approach would not have seemed so bad to her before she met Joe.

Joe had changed things.

And now she was going to him.

She took a breath. Her safety belt was fastened still, although the plane was airborne now. Any moment the NO SMOKING and FASTEN BELTS signs would go out. She wished they would hurry about it. She wanted a cigarette. The belt didn't bother her—she would leave it on until they landed, since it didn't limit her in any way. But she did want a cigarette.

She glanced out the window, looking out to see what the ground looked like, but the wing was in the way. She looked straight out instead and saw the sky. It wasn't blue when you were in the middle of it. It was just air. And the clouds, when you came upon them, were not snowy puffs of cotton (or, for that matter, cottony puffs of snow) the way they were from the ground. Just steam from a kettle, or a low fog, or something of the sort. They didn't look like clouds at all.

Funny.

One of the stewardesses, the short dark one, came around with magazines. Marilyn shook her head. The signs were off now and she looked through her purse for a cigarette. She found one, lit it. She was travelling light. Just the purse and a single suitcase, that was all. But the rest of her belongings were packed and ready to go. Sandstone was awaiting word. One telegram from Marilyn and Railway Express would come by to carry them wherever Marilyn wanted them carried.

To Kansas City.

That was the idea. She was going to him, going to stay, but she was not sure that he would want her. There was no denying the fact that he had wanted her very much when he was in New York. And he had not been lying—he had wanted her, not for one weekend or one week, but forever.

Did he still want her forever?

It was doubtful. He was not in New York now but in Kansas City. Love is love anywhere, but Kansas City and New York were two different worlds. She might fit into his life neatly enough in New York and be a stranger in his home town.

These were things she would have to find out.

Time passed. She thought about New York, and the job she had left, and the apartment she would not be living in any more. She thought about Saundra and Joan, and she thought about the people at Phulcorte, and she realized that she would in all probability never see any of those people again. She thought about all the men—too many of them—that she had slept with. They did not matter anymore. She tried to remember them and was surprised to discover that she could not remember any of them clearly, could not draw the mental pictures of their individual faces into focus. They were all blurred.

Joe had shoved them into the shadows. They were unimportant now. He was important, the only person who mattered in her life. So they ceased to exist. A part of a life she was no longer living. A remnant of another Marilyn Harper. No kin of hers, that girl. No relative.

Then, almost before she knew it, the signs were on. NO SMOKING. FASTEN BELTS. She squashed the cigarette she was smoking, checked to assure herself that her belt had not come unfastened, and tensed herself for landing. The landing was a long time in coming. It was silk smooth. There was the slightest bump when they touched down, then no jolt at all after it.

They were on the ground.

In Kansas City airport.

She left the plane, went into the terminal, waited to pick up her luggage at the baggage counter, then checked a phone book for the numbers of Joe's stores. One of them seemed to be the main store and she called it first. He wasn't in, the clerk informed her, not just then. Out To Lunch. He'd be in; fifteen minutes or so.

She thanked the clerk and rang off. There was a limousine waiting to take passengers into the center of town but she decided to save time by taking a cab. The cab ran almost three dollars with tip but let her off in front of the store.

She walked inside. She asked a clerk if Mr. Jeffers was around. Not just yet, the clerk said. Out To Lunch. Any minute though—

She said she would wait. She walked around the store, a neat trim brunette in a neatly-tailored dark green suit, looking at football helmets and catcher's mitts and golf clubs and basketballs and tennis rackets. It was a big store. It seemed to have everything she could imagine. Fishing tackle, hunting jackets, rifles, skin diving gear—

And then Joe came through the front door.

He saw her, and she saw the look in his eyes, and she knew he could not believe it, and he was rushing across the store, racing down the aisle, and she was running to meet him, and she was in his arms and he was holding her, almost crushing her, his mouth to hers and his arm tight around her.

The clerks were a bit shocked.

"I knew you'd come," he told her. "I . . . you had to come. I needed you so much."

"You didn't write."

"I had to give you time. Time to make up your mind. I couldn't push you. Marilyn. It wouldn't have worked if I had pushed you."

"Well, I'm here."

"For good?"

"If you still want me."

"Of course I want you—"

"Tell me."

"I want you. I love you. What more?"

"Now kiss me, Joe."

He kissed her, and in the middle of the third aisle her

mouth opened for him and his tongue went into her mouth and she pressed her body against him. His hands roamed her back and she felt passion flare up within her body, a living thing, burning her insides with its savage ferocity.

"Any minute now," she said. "Any minute and we're going to be down on the floor. Right in the middle of the aisle. Our clothes off and you inside of me and—"

"Sounds good."

"Bad for business."

"Don't be silly. They can sell tickets."

"Joe—"

"Let's get out of here," he said. "Let's take the afternoon off, you and me. Let's go to City Hall for blood tests. There's a two-day waiting period, we can't be married today. We can have a honeymoon, though. One now, one after the wedding. How does that sound?"

It sounded fine.

It was even better than it sounded.

IN A FURNISHED apartment on West 100th Street, a young man named Michael Gleit sat in front of a telephone. He was looking at a slip of paper with a name and a number on it. He looked at the name and number for several minutes, nervously shaping phrases in his mind.

Then he lifted the receiver and dialed the number. OXford 9-5982, he dialed.

Then he sat chewing his nails.

In another apartment on the other side of town—on the twelfth floor to be precise—the telephone rang. A very pretty redhead girl wearing white short-shorts and a blue jersey tee-shirt answered the phone. She picked up the receiver and sat down on the couch.

"Hello," she said. "Who's this?"

"Uh," the man said. "Uh . . . is this Saundra?"

"Uh-huh."

"This is . . . uh . . . this is a friend of Frank's."

"Frank?"

"Frank," the man said. "You know. Frank Ralston."

"Oh," Sandstone said. "*That* Frank."

"Yeah."

"Well, naturally, any friend of Frank's is a friend of mine. Can I help you, friend?"

There was a moment of silence.

"Uh . . . Frank said—"

"He was telling the truth."

"Uh . . . are you free tomorrow night?"

"What's wrong with tonight, friend?"

"Tonight?"

"Why not?"

"Well," the man said. "Uh . . . nothing's wrong. I mean—"

"Got the address?"

"No."

She gave him the address and told him to hurry. Just thinking about it was getting to her and she hoped that it would be nice with him, that he was a nice guy.

She put the receiver back on the hook and lay down on the couch. She sighed, hoping the phone company would let her keep the same phone number when she moved to another apartment. And she would have to move soon. For one thing, with Marilyn gone for keeps, the place was just too damn big. And the rent was too steep for Joan when it was split two ways. The kid couldn't make it, and Sandstone was damned if she was going to pay that kind of rent all by herself.

She'd get a small place all her own, two rooms and a kitchen somewhere on the East Side. A good place, too. She could afford a hundred fifty a month if she had to pay that much. She was making more money than she knew what to do with.

But it would be good if she could keep the same phone number. The number was just beginning to get into circulation, and it would be a pain in the neck if they changed it.

Soon she would quit her job. She still had it—it seemed important to have some kind of respectable front. But there was a better out that she had read about, one that wouldn't force her to get up in the morning. There was this model agency that let you register with it for twenty dollars a month. They didn't get you any work, but they listed you on the books so that you had a respectable job in case anybody got nosey. That made sense, and pretty soon she'd tell Caution Insurance to go to the devil and hook up with the paper agency.

She smiled.

She was a very happy girl. Genuinely happy—and how many girls could make that statement? Not many, she thought. Not many at all.

Marilyn could, of course. Marilyn was no longer Marilyn Harper. She was now Marilyn Jeffers according to the telegram. Married and ready to settle down.

It seemed incredible.

Marilyn was the career woman, the one who was going to set a fire on Publisher's Row. So now Marilyn had bid a fond adieu to Publisher's Row and had married the owner of a chain of sporting goods stores and was living the good life in Kansas City, which was a long ways indeed from Publisher's Row.

Weird.

Whereas Saundra Stone, who had planned on hooking a well-off husband had wound up in Marilyn's shoes. Now she *was* a career woman, with a well-paying job which she enjoyed, and wasn't that a cock-eyed turn of events?

It was indeed.

She sighed. Soon, she thought, the customer would arrive. She limited herself to one customer a day for the time being, and she charged each customer twenty-five dollars. The price had gone up since Frank became the first paying customer. Outside of Johnny Lipton, of course. He was different. She hadn't set a price; he'd made his own.

But, when she wasn't working anymore, then she could re-arrange her schedule. Maybe take a customer each afternoon and another each night—that might be a good idea. And set up a special scale. A customer who stayed all night should pay more than one who left after a brief roll in the hay.

Say, fifty bucks for the night, twenty-five for a single piece.

That made sense. And it wasn't too high a price. Hell, beasts who walked the streets charged ten or fifteen. And they couldn't compare with her.

The bell rang.

She walked to the door, opened it. The man was not the best specimen of humanity upon which she had ever set eyes. He was thin and short, with a weak chin and thick eyeglasses. But he looked like a pretty nice guy.

"Hi," she said happily. "Come on inside. I'm Saundra."

"I'm . . . uh . . . Walter."

"Walter? Should I call you Walter or Walt?" He looked more like a Walter than a Walt, she thought. But you could never tell about such matters.

"Walt," he said.

"Care for a drink, Walt?"

He nodded gratefully. She mixed two bourbon highballs, gave him one, and clinked glasses with him. They drank, and they sat together on the couch, and the drink seemed to loosen him up. He unwound a bit.

"I'm afraid I have to talk about money, Walt," she said, her tone carefully apologetic. "Would you like to stay all night or leave right away? It's twenty-five for just once or fifty for all night."

She was sure he was a one-shot man. He surprised her, taking his wallet from his inside jacket pocket, finding a fifty dollar bill, handing it to her. She put the money away and returned to him.

She reached for him, took his face in her hands, kissed him. She took off his glasses and set them carefully on the table at the side of the couch. She kissed him again. He looked much better without the glasses. They had an owlish effect. He was far more forceful and masculine in appearance without them.

She sat up, threw her shoulders back so that her breasts were outlined against the jersey tee-shirt. She was not wearing a bra and the nipples were plainly visible.

"Do you like my breasts, Walt?"

"Very much."

"Touch them."

He touched them gingerly, cupping from underneath, lifting them and feeling their weight. She saw passion in his eyes. He was a frightened little man, she knew, but she knew also that she had what it would take to dispel his fears.

"Take my shirt off, Walt."

She lifted up her arms and he pulled the tee-shirt over her head. Her breasts were bare now and she heard the sudden intake of breath as he caught sight of their naked splendor. Very hesitantly he reached out to touch one breast. His fingers were very cool on her flesh and they set her on fire. He played with her nipples and she began to tingle with desire.

"The bedroom," she said softly. "Let's go to the bedroom, Walt. Let's go to bed together, Walt. I like you. I like you, Walt. Come to bed with me."

She took him by the hand and led the way to her bedroom. The bed was ready for action, almost vulgar in its appearance.

It was all made up, but the sheet was drawn back in such a way as to invite anyone visiting the room to get into the bed.

That was the general idea.

"Take off my shorts, Walt. Take then, off, baby. I'm not wearing any panties. There's just me under the shorts, Walt, just me, and I'm all warm for you, all aching for you. Take off the shorts, Walt."

This, she knew, was the right way with the frightened ones. Make them do all the work. Let them think they were the dominant ones, sitting in the driver's seat and making her quiver like a jellyfish. As a matter of complete fact, she was indeed quivering like a jellyfish.

But that was beside the point.

Now Walt, dear old Walt, was removing his own clothes. She was not too much surprised to discover that he was as much a man as many stronger-looking guys. It often worked that way.

He took her in his arms. He stroked her breasts, then reached down to draw her close to him. She moved against him, felt him grow with desire for her.

She blew gently into his ear, kissed the ear and the side of his throat.

She rubbed her breasts against his chest.

She kissed him.

"I need you, Walt. I need you. I need you so much I'm going crazy. Oh, I want you, Walt. Hurry, hurry, baby, do it, baby, do it—"

They tumbled together to the bed.

And then it began. He had trouble finding the right place, but she was skillful, taking the situation in hand, and from that point on everything was under control.

The world began to race by and she knew that it was going to happen. It was amazing the way it worked for her. It wasn't supposed to—according to everything she had ever heard or read, a prostitute did not enjoy her customers.

This was not the case with Saundra Stone, not by any stretch of the imagination.

She enjoyed everything.

All the time.

And she was certainly a prostitute. She didn't hate the label. There was a play she had read in school entitled *The Respectable Prostitute*. That was how she thought of herself. She was respectable and she was a prostitute. Period.

It was getting better and better now. It was getting very good indeed, and the world was turning and her arms were around Walter and her breasts were flattened out against his chest and it was good, so very good!

No career woman in the history of the world ever enjoyed her job more.

THE BRUNETTE WITH the very pale skin was excited.

There, now. Doesn't that sound like a sentence from a high school French-language textbook? The fountain pen of my aunt is on the bureau of my uncle. The man with brown walking-shoes was sitting in the garden. The brunette with the very pale skin was excited.

Well, she was. The brunette with the very pale skin was about as excited as one can get, and that's saying a lot. Quite a lot.

They had met in Washington Square Park. The brunette with the very pale skin had been walking down the wide asphalt path that runs from the Circle to the tables, where old men play chess and checkers, and she had seen this blonde, and something had clicked. It was that sort of thing. Spontaneous, because it clicked for both of them at once. Wordless, because words of any sort were quite unnecessary.

They exchanged glances—*locked eyes* might be a more accurate way of stating it. Then the blonde had stood up—a beautiful girl, a magnificent body—and they walked together, heading automatically for the apartment of the brunette with the very pale skin.

Which was located at 89 Barrow Street.

They were in that apartment now. There was a bed in that apartment, and they were on top of it. Before they had sat listening silently to a Haydn quartet, and they had had Vat 69 Scotch which they drank out of paper cups, and then they had taken off their clothes. Now they were quite naked, and they were together, and they were on the bed.

And the brunette with the very pale skin was excited.

So was the blonde.

They were in a very strange position. They were kissing

mouth-to-mouth and yet their feet were at opposite ends of the bed. The brunette had a very long bed. The blonde lay on her back at one end of it, and the brunette lay on her stomach at the other end of it, and their heads met in the middle, and they were kissing.

Passionately.

They began to move at once.

The brunette shifted slightly, and her lips touched the chin of the blonde. She kissed the blonde's chin, and the blonde kissed her chin, and they kept going.

Now the brunette was nibbling the blonde's throat. The blonde had very soft skin, and the brunette's little pink tongue shot out and coursed over the skin, and the blonde reciprocated by doing much the same thing to the brunette.

They wiggled together.

The blonde had beautiful breasts that stood up straight and proud from her chest. Small light brown aureoles surrounding beautiful coral nipples. Very beautiful breasts.

The brunette kissed them.

First one and then the other.

They worked on each other for ten minutes that seemed more like ten hours.

But after ten minutes of this they began to look for other fascinating things. They moved very slowly, and they kissed each other and they kept looking.

And found what they were looking for.

Oh, they found it all right.

And were delighted with what they found. The blonde was delighted, and the brunette was delighted, and what more could they ask for?

And this, too, went on for a long time. And got better, and better, and better and better and better, driving upward at an incredible speed, whirling and sailing dizzily, crescendoing into the very stratosphere, reaching the absolute heights.

The top—

And much later, much much later, the brunette rolled over onto her side and moaned deliciously. And long after that she managed to speak.

"I'm Carole," she said. "Carole Clark."

"I'm Joan," the blonde girl said.

"Joan—"

"Joan McKay," the blonde girl said.

MY NEWSLETTER: I get out an email newsletter at unpredictable intervals, but rarely more often than every other week. I'll be happy to add you to the distribution list. A blank email to lawbloc@gmail.com with "newsletter" in the subject line will get you on the list, and a click of the "Unsubscribe" link will get you off it, should you ultimately decide you're happier without it.

LAWRENCE BLOCK is a Mystery Writers of America Grand Master. His work over the past half century has earned him multiple Edgar Allan Poe and Shamus awards, the U.K. Diamond Dagger for lifetime achievement, and recognition in Germany, France, Taiwan, and Japan. His latest novel is *Dead Girl Blues*; other recent fiction includes *A Time to Scatter Stones, Keller's Fedora*, and *The Burglar in Short Order*. In addition to novels and short fiction, he has written episodic television (*Tilt!*) and the Wong Kar-wai film, *My Blueberry Nights*.

Block contributed a fiction column in Writer's Digest for fourteen years, and has published several books for writers, including the classic *Telling Lies for Fun & Profit* and the updated and expanded *Writing the Novel from Plot to Print to Pixel*. His nonfiction has been collected in *The Crime of Our Lives* (about mystery fiction) and *Hunting Buffalo with Bent Nails* (about everything else). Most recently, his collection of columns about stamp collecting, *Generally Speaking*, has found a substantial audience throughout and far beyond the philatelic community.

Lawrence Block has lately found a new career as an anthologist (*At Home in the Dark; From Sea to Stormy Sea*) and holds the position of writer-in-residence at South Carolina's Newberry College. He is a modest and humble fellow, although you would never guess as much from this biographical note.

Email: lawbloc@gmail.com
Twitter: @LawrenceBlock
Facebook: lawrence.block
Website: lawrenceblock.com